In front of the goal, [...]
Escaping the keeper's [...]
ricocheted off the cr[...]
slashed reflexively at t[...]

'*Yeees!*'

'*Lovely!*'

Flint had barely slid to a halt when a hand tugged roughly at his collar. He rolled over on his back.

'*Idiot!* Didn't you hear me call?' Aldo spat with rage. 'That was *my* ball!'

'Says?' Flint leapt to his feet. 'You had your chance! You missed!'

Aldo's scowl was ugly. 'You were in my way!' He pushed Flint backwards.

Fists clenched, Flint returned the shove . . .

Also available by Neil Arksey, and
published by Corgi Yearling Books:

BROOKSIE
FLINT

SUDDEN DEATH
NEIL ARKSEY

CORGI YEARLING BOOKS

SUDDEN DEATH
A CORGI YEARLING BOOK : 0 440 864461

First publication in Great Britain

PRINTING HISTORY
Corgi Yearling edition published 2001

1 3 5 7 9 10 8 6 4 2

Copyright © 2001 by Neil Arksey

The right of Neil Arksey to be identified as the author of this work has been asserted in accordance with the Copyright, Designs and Patents Act 1988

Condition of Sale
This book is sold subject to the condition that it shall not, by way of trade or otherwise, be lent, re-sold, hired out or otherwise circulated without the publisher's prior consent in any form of binding or cover other than that in which it is published and without a similar condition including this condition being imposed on the subsequent purchaser.

Set in 13/15pt New Century Schoolbook by
Phoenix Typesetting, Ilkley, West Yorkshire

Corgi Yearling Books are published by Transworld Publishers,
61–63 Uxbridge Road, London W5 5SA,
a division of The Random House Group Ltd,
in Australia by Random House Australia (Pty) Ltd,
20 Alfred Street, Milsons Point, NSW 2061, Australia,
in New Zealand by Random House New Zealand Ltd,
18 Poland Road, Glenfield, Auckland 10, New Zealand,
and in South Africa by Random House (Pty) Ltd,
Endulini, 5a Jubilee Road, Parktown 2193, South Africa.

The Random House Group Limited supports The Forest Stewardship Council® (FSC®), the leading international forest-certification organisation. Our books carrying the FSC label are printed on FSC®-certified paper. FSC is the only forest-certification scheme supported by the leading environmental organisations, including Greenpeace. Our paper procurement policy can be found at www.randomhouse.co.uk/environment

MIX
Paper from
responsible sources
FSC
www.fsc.org FSC® C016897

Printed and bound in Great Britain by Clays Ltd, St Ives PLC

CHAPTER 1
A PROMISING START

Beneath the bonnet the cooling engine ticked. Leaning out of the window, Flint sniffed the air. It smelt fresh; it smelt of trees. The neat quiet street felt friendly, welcoming; the gardens looked cared for and the houses were pretty.

'This isn't quite how things are supposed to happen.' Reaching over to the back seat, Sandra, his keyworker, grabbed a file. 'But as you're such a balanced young man . . .' She raised an eyebrow. '. . . And because the Bakers are so well known to us, I'm bending the rules. Speeding things up.'

Sandra hated having to do things by the book, four months at the children's home had taught Flint that. There was a streak in her. She'd been a bit of a rebel in her time, you could tell. She had been in 'care' herself she had once told him, she knew how it could make you feel. That's what made her good at her job. He liked her. He was lucky to have her.

She rummaged through the pages. 'There's some pictures here somewhere – I should have given them to you days ago.'

'No need.' Flint's tone was matter of fact. 'Already seen them.'

'What!' Sandra hugged the file to her chest. 'You can't have! This stuff's meant to be . . .' The warm dark of her eyes dilated, accusatory. 'Oh, I hope you haven't been . . .'

Flint scowled. She didn't need to say it. He knew exactly what she was thinking. She knew all about him and his past: his dad sent down for a string of thefts, his own participation in the breaking and entering. 'What do you take me for?'

'How else could you have seen the photos?'

'I haven't. I saw *them*.'

'Mr and Mrs Baker?'

Flint nodded.

'In the flesh?'

Flint couldn't resist a smirk. 'So to speak!'

'But . . .'

'They're getting on a bit,' said Flint. 'Both of them. He smiles a lot. His hair, what's left of it, is going grey. None of that combing-it-over nonsense. He keeps it short. She's thin and stricter looking. Her hair is dark. He's got an accent, from somewhere up north.' Flint grinned – Sandra recognized the picture he was painting. 'They hold hands.'

'I don't understand.' Sandra's brow furrowed. 'When did you see them?'

Flint chuckled. 'Can't you guess?'

The frown deepened. 'No.' Impatient. 'Tell me.'

'Mickey D's.'

Sandra's face fell. 'McDonald's? Our little trip?'

'We're not thick, you know.' Flint scowled. 'Credit us with a bit more intelligence. How often do we get taken to McDonald's on a one-to-one? Every kid in the home has worked that one out. It's what you lot call a "blind visit".'

Sandra sighed. 'Is there anything we can keep from you kids?'

Flint smiled. 'We've got ears, we don't need to pry.'

'OK, Mr Smartypants.' Sandra glanced across at the neat terraced house. 'So you're ready for this?'

Flint nodded. 'Totally.'

'Anything else you want to ask?'

Flint shook his head.

'Hmm . . .' Sandra looked him up and down. 'Fairly presentable.' Licking her thumbs she reached over.

Flint squirmed and tried to dodge her grasp, but she gripped him firmly. It was a little game between them – the slicking down of the eyebrows.

'Come on, you want to look your best.' Sandra smiled. 'There! Angelic!'

'OK.' Flint yanked open the car door and scrambled out. 'Let's do it!'

'Pleased to meet you.' Mrs Baker – Janet, as she'd just introduced herself – shook Flint's hand firmly and peered. Not unfriendly, but scrutinizing. The lines around her eyes and mouth deepened and darkened when she smiled.

Flint wondered if Janet dyed her hair – she looked even older at close range. He smiled back. 'Everyone calls me Flint.'

Her husband chuckled and held out his hand. 'Everyone calls me Jim.' The shake was vigorous. His feet shuffled nervously.

After a few minutes of awkward small talk, Sandra suggested Janet take her for a look round the house. Jim volunteered to make some tea and show Flint the garden.

In the kitchen, Jim winked conspiratorially as he filled the kettle. 'The ladies enjoy a little natter.' He motioned towards the garden. 'It's not massive, but there's a good-sized lawn. Janet's the gardener. I mow, under orders. Want to take a look?'

Flint nodded.

Jim led him out onto a small patio. 'Our lads are grown now. But when they were younger they used to make a right old mess of it, kicking a ball around.'

The lawn was lush but closely cropped, surrounded on three sides by beds of plants and a wooden fence. At the far end was a shed; it had seen better days. Flint stared at the neat grass.

'Come with me.' Jim set off across the lawn. 'If Janet had her way no-one would ever walk on it.' He chuckled. 'She's getting a bit pernickety in her old age. She'd get rid of that too,' he grumbled, nodding towards the shed. 'Calls it "The Eyesore".'

Treading lightly, Flint followed across the lawn. It felt like luxury carpet underfoot.

'Heh . . .' Jim stopped and turned. 'What should a team do if the pitch is flooded?'

Flint shrugged. 'Abandon the match?'

Jim shook his head. A broad grin spread across his face. 'Bring on their subs of course!'

Flint laughed.

'Like that, did you?'

Flint nodded. A promising start.

Unlocking the shed, Jim stepped inside. When he reappeared moments later he was still smiling. He held a football in his hands. 'You like a kick too, I understand?'

They had clicked, just like that: Jim had chipped him the ball, he had headed it back . . .

'Good . . . a little lower . . . on the brow . . . good, and again . . . good! OK, now let's try a little footwork . . .'

Instant understanding.

They had been working on shooting technique when Janet finally emerged onto the patio with Sandra. 'So much for you two making the tea – there's more to it than just switching on the kettle you know!

It's brewing now. Come and join us in the front room. Cake.'

Chocolate cake. Rich and moist. Munching his way through a third slice, Flint was feeling about as good as he could remember.

'Football's a bit of a passion of mine,' said Jim.

Janet shook her head. 'Obsession, more like.'

'I coach a youth team,' said Jim. 'Welbeck YFC.'

'Evenings and weekends I scarcely see him,' said Janet. 'If Jim didn't have to earn, he'd give up plastering like a shot and spend his whole life down there.'

'We carry out most of our trials at the start of the season,' said Jim. 'But if you're interested, maybe I could arrange a try-out for you.'

Flint felt his heart race.

Smiling warmly, Sandra nodded towards Flint. 'I can't think of anything that would make this one happier. At Bella Gardens he's forever nagging the kids and pestering the staff to give him a game.'

'If Jim and Janet say yes, how long will

I have to wait before I can move in?' asked Flint.

'Well . . .' Glancing from Janet to Jim, Sandra smiled diplomatically. 'There's a format we have to follow – there would normally be several more meetings like this one.'

'More football, tea and cake?'

'Perhaps.' Sandra shrugged. 'We normally ask prospective parents to come up and visit Bella Gardens. Then we try to arrange for a couple of meetings in more neutral places. To find out how you guys get on in different settings.'

'Might take some time then?' Flint's tone betrayed his disappointment.

Sandra glanced again at Jim and Janet. They smiled. She smiled. 'Let's see.'

CHAPTER 2
DERELICT

'Must have been someone's home once.'

Flint nodded. 'Some lucky family.'

Surrounded by overgrown trees and bushes, the house stood alone at the end of the street, dark and derelict. It was huge – barely smaller than Bella Gardens, which he shared with twelve other kids and a crew of careworkers.

At a gap in the fence where planks had been smashed, Flint thrust his hand through into the dense foliage. The branches pressed against the fence with such force that one day soon they would push it over. Taking firm hold on a branch, he ducked his head, shielded his face, and shoved through. The foliage jabbed, poked and resisted, but he turned so his back took the brunt. Shove by shove, he bulldozed an opening.

'Thanks!' Slipping through behind him, Beanie dropped low and scrambled to where a path of sorts had been hacked. Flint followed after her. He was taller than her and several times had to scramble on his hands and knees to get past low obstructions.

'Hey, Bean!' A whistle and a shout rang out from above. Beanie's trademark red woollen hat was recognizable even beneath the trees and bushes. Two figures, fuzzily visible through the foliage, leant and peered from an upstairs window. 'Who's that with you?'

'My mate, Flint.'

The tunnel through the overgrown garden led to where there had once been a ground-floor window. Now it was just a gaping rectangular hole. Following Beanie, Flint scrambled up onto the rough ledge and dropped into darkness.

With so little light, sight became redundant. The other senses – hearing, touch, smell – sharpened. Laughter and distorted voices echoed through the empty house. Strong sour smells pervaded the gloom.

Treading carefully, Flint followed Beanie's dark shape amongst discarded cans and broken furniture, through to the hall and staircase. Against the dim light from the holed roof, figures stood silhouetted on the landing.

'Watch yerselves!' Flint recognized the cynical laugh – *Stretch*. 'There's another stair gone. Fifth from the top.'

Beanie grunted. 'Fat lot of help! How many from the bottom?'

'Didn't count.' Stretch chuckled. 'Can't miss it though – there's a great big hole. Some of the other steps didn't feel too solid neither.'

Flint nudged Beanie. She knew the stairs much better than him. 'After you.'

'Stuff your chivalry!' said Beanie. 'I'm bringing up the rear.'

Laughter from above filled the empty hall.

'If the stairs take your weight,' said Beanie, 'they'll take mine. If not . . .' She shrugged. 'One more hole for me to jump.' She gave him a sharp shove. 'Up you go. First gap's number seven.'

Flint climbed close to the wall – there was no banister. He moved quickly to the first gap, stretched over it, then advanced upwards one step at a time, testing each step before he gave it his full weight. The boys on the landing added their commentary.

'Oooh, careful now . . . that one sounds a bit dodgy.'

'Easy does it!'

Flint pressed himself tight to the wall and kept his weight to the edge. With Beanie close behind and the boys watching from above there was pressure not to hesitate or falter. But three quarters of the way up, he spotted the gaping hole. A second rotten stair completely disintegrated. He peered into the gloom: it was a *long* way down.

'Come on!' urged Beanie from behind.

'Nearly there!' Stretch's lopsided grin loomed; blunt ugly features exaggerated by dim light. 'Sprint it!'

Glancing down into the dark hall below, Flint steeled himself. *It couldn't be so dangerous . . . the others had all managed.* Taking a deep breath, he sprang, cleared the gap and scuttled up the last few steps.

Beanie skipped in effortlessly behind. 'You took your time.'

Stretch and his two mates slapped palms and touched knuckles with Beanie, a ritual handshake Flint had come to associate with this new world. He recognized the two boys: Nidge, hovering like some skinny ghost, and behind him one of the dark-skinned, almond-eyed twins. Jumbled voices rolled along the landing.

'How you doing, little friend.' Stretch grinned at Beanie, nodded to Flint. 'Through here.' As he turned, his skull caught the light, it gleamed like the toe of a polished boot.

At the far end of the landing, a big empty shell of a room, like all the other rooms stripped of its fittings, its walls layered in graffiti. Boys were slumped on broken sofas, others stood smoking by the window or crouched in corners. Laughter, chatter and the tiny whispered tunes of personal stereos filled the room. Flint nodded to faces he recognized. Lost boys, from who knows where. Some in 'care' with local authority children's homes; others preferring to take their chances.

'We was wondering if you'd show.' Stretch took a cigarette from a packet then offered them.

Beanie reached out eagerly to take one.

Flint scowled and shook his head.

Lighting their cigarettes, Stretch

grinned through blue smoke. 'Don't want to clog up those squeaky clean lungs, eh?'

Flint shrugged. 'Smoking's a mug's game.'

Beanie coughed, choked and snorted, her eyes watered. There were sniggers from the sofas, but she took another drag and held it down.

'So how's things at Bella?'

'Same as ever.' Beanie puffed and made clouds of smoke, ignoring Flint's disapproving gaze. A mischievous twinkle appeared in her eye. 'Flint's been to Mickey D's.'

'Blind visit – yeah?' Stretch turned to the sofas. 'D'you hear that, you lot?'

Flint felt himself tensing. A lot of the boys had been in children's homes. Most knew the system – careworkers arranged a blind visit so prospective foster parents could check you out. He hadn't told Beanie he'd reached the next stage, a visit to the parents at their house.

'Pretty boy here's had a vetting.' Stretch patted Flint on the shoulder. 'Congratulations!' Stretch didn't think much of the procedure. Chuckles around the room echoed his cynicism.

Flint shrugged. Blind visits were kind of degrading, but if you wanted to live in a home with a mum and dad and maybe brothers, sisters and pets – not an institution with curfews, fire alarms and reinforced windows – they were one of the hoops you had to jump through. 'Probably won't come to anything,' he muttered, crossing his fingers and hoping like hell that it would. Some of the doubters around him had probably had their hopes dashed after just such a visit. Maybe more than once. He knew he was lucky to be through to the next round.

Flint coughed. The smoke was making his throat dry. Scanning the room he spotted the football in the corner. 'So what about this game, then?'

His question was greeted with a cacophony of *yeahs*, groans and sniggers. Some of the boys had got to their feet. There was a buzz of excitement.

'This boy's keen!' Taking a final drag, Stretch flicked his cigarette, picked up the football and squeezed it between his palms – it wheezed and crumpled. He tossed the useless carcass at Flint. 'Punctured.'

'No problem,' said Flint. 'The other side'll have one.'

'Maybe.' Stretch clapped his hands. 'Come on, you lazy dossers!' he barked, heading for the door. 'Time we got a new ball. Let's shop!'

CHAPTER 3
SHOPPING

Music pumped out through the *Sports Emporium* doorway. Hard, fast, loud. Flint, Beanie and the twins, Clifton and Carlton, strode through the entrance swaggering in time to the beat. Ahead of them, Stretch, Nidge and another boy were making their way down one of the brightly lit aisles. Stretch paused to examine a trainer on display. His two companions peeled away and drifted off through the store.

Stretch put two fingers in his mouth and whistled shrill enough to cut through the pounding music and catch the attention of an assistant hovering by the central tills. The assistant made his way over. Stretch held the trainer aloft. 'Got one of these in a size three?'

The assistant frowned as he approached. 'Three?'

Stretch laughed. 'Not for me, stupid!' He nodded towards Beanie. 'The girl.' Waving the trainer under Beanie's nose, Stretch thrust it into the assistant's surprised hands. 'And while you're at it . . .' He reached and snatched another trainer from a higher shelf. 'Got a pair of these in a seven?'

The trainer flew through the air. The assistant lunged to catch it.

'What about you?' Stretch patted one of the twins on the arm. 'See anything you fancy?'

The boy – Clifton or Carlton, Flint couldn't tell them apart – looked puzzled.

Stretch nudged him and nodded towards the assistant. 'Come on. He may as well get several pairs whilst he's at it.'

The boy turned his attention to the shelves of trainers. 'Yeah . . .' He grabbed an expensive-looking model. 'How about one of these. Size six.'

With three trainers in his arms, the flustered assistant headed off towards the storeroom.

Stretch chuckled. 'That should keep him busy for a while.' He turned, surveying the store. 'Right, spread out and see how many others you can distract.'

The group split. With an uneasy feeling, Flint followed Beanie to the section of the shop where replica football shirts were on display. The latest kit for each Premiership team and many of the more popular league sides hung on racks, covering an entire wall.

'What's going on?' hissed Flint.

'You'll see!' Beanie grinned. Making her way to where last season's shirts were on sale at reduced prices, she tugged at a Man United shirt. 'Look at the price on this!' Manchester United were Beanie's team. She frowned, outraged. 'They're taking liberties. Last year's shirt! How can anyone afford them?' She beckoned to a female shop assistant. 'This can't be right.'

The assistant peered at the price tag. She shrugged. 'That's the price.'

'Talk about daylight robbery,' snapped Beanie.

The uneasy assistant forced a placating smile.

Flint's gaze drifted past the assistant, down the aisle between the racks of clothes. At the far end, Stretch suddenly appeared. Nidge followed behind, carrying a sports bag. The two of them marched swiftly towards a bin full of footballs. Flint glanced at Beanie.

Beanie was tugging at the price tag on an offending shirt. 'Look at this!' she ranted. 'It's *criminal*!'

The assistant seemed uncertain how to respond to a girl half her size and age coming on like an irate adult. 'There are cheaper shirts in the T-shirt section.'

'The T-shirt section?' Beanie scowled. 'The T-shirt section? That's not a lot of good is it! I'm a Man U supporter.'

The assistant shrugged again. 'Man United T-shirts?'

Flint felt his skin prickle. Stretch was pushing the second of two footballs into the sports bag held open by Nidge. The two of them kept glancing around, checking for watching eyes. They were *stealing*.

'If you want to speak to the manager . . . ?' Growing irritable, the assistant glared at Beanie. Enough was enough. 'I'll find him for you.' She turned.

Beanie lunged. 'No!'

The assistant glowered at the hand gripping her sleeve. Up the aisle behind her, Stretch struggled with the sports bag's zip.

Beanie let go. 'There's no need,' she said softly. 'Point me in the direction of the T-shirt section, I'll take a look.' She beamed an angelic smile, a polite little girl. 'You never know, something might take my fancy.'

The assistant pointed. 'T-shirts are over there.'

Flint breathed a sigh of relief.

With the sports bag zipped shut, casual as anything, Stretch and Nidge walked past. Stretch shot Beanie a sly wink.

Flint's pulse was suddenly racing. His face and ears felt hot. He knew he must be blushing.

'Come on!' Beanie tugged at his elbow. 'T-shirts.'

Flint felt the assistant's suspicious gaze as they made their way between the racks of shorts and shirts. Hairs prickled on the back of his neck. His palms were sweating.

Beanie stopped by a rack of T-shirts, still acting the interested shopper. 'What d'you reckon?' She fingered a red and white T-shirt bearing the words MANCHESTER UNITED above a small crest.

Flint tried to concentrate on the T-shirt, but his gaze kept pulling back towards the assistant. She was walking towards them. The blood was pounding so loudly in his ears he was certain she would hear. In the distance the twins nonchalantly made their way towards the exit. Beanie spotted them too. The gang were leaving.

'Like to try one on?' asked the assistant condescendingly.

Beanie smiled sourly back. 'No.' She yanked at the T-shirt, pulling it from its hanger. 'This is offensive.' She flung the shirt at the assistant. 'They haven't even got the logo right.'

As the shirt dropped to the floor, the assistant glared and bent to retrieve it.

Beanie gave Flint a sharp nudge. 'Come on! We're wasting our time in this dump.' She turned and headed for the exit.

With his heart in his mouth, Flint hurried after her. He grabbed her arm. 'You saw what they just did?'

'Of course.' Beanie frowned.

'You were helping.'

'So were you!' Beanie chuckled. 'What's the problem? This place is robbing people all day long.'

The shrill whine of a security alarm cut

through the beat of the music. Shoppers turned. But Stretch and his cohorts were already vanishing into the crowded mall.

'Quick!' Beanie tugged at Flint's sleeve. *'Scarper!'*

CHAPTER 4
CHASE

Stretch and Nidge had halted by stairs to catch their breath and check for pursuers. Flint and Beanie caught up, panting. Other familiar faces emerged from the crowd. The gang that had set off from the house was regrouping.

And a bottleneck was forming. Shoppers muttered and scowled disapprovingly as they queued to squeeze by.

Stretch's laugh was defiant. 'That security guard was never going to catch us.'

Nidge nodded. 'Way too old!'

'And fat!' Stretch snatched the sports bag from Nidge, unzipped it and showed the others. 'See? Liberated!'

Beanie nudged Flint. 'Now we've got our ball to play with.'

'Two, as a matter of fact.' Stretch grinned at Flint. 'What's up? You don't look happy.'

Flint didn't feel like smiling. Loitering with a bunch of gung-ho, bragging shoplifters was the last thing he should be doing. If he got nicked, it would go straight on his file – that would look good beside the stuff about the burglaries and his father doing time – and he could kiss being fostered goodbye. He scowled. 'You never said this was what you meant by "shopping".'

Stretch's eyes challenged. 'So?'

Flint looked away, his eyes scanning the crowd for signs of uniform.

Stretch grinned and nudged Beanie. 'I don't think your mate approves.' The grin vanished. 'Raass!' The eyes narrowed, the face darkened. 'Trouble coming! *Split!*'

Flint jerked round. The uniformed cap of the shop's security guard was bobbing towards them through the sea of heads. But there were other uniforms: mall security guards, two looking down from the upper floor, more advancing through the shoppers, grim-faced men with frowns on their faces and walkie-talkies clutched to their mouths.

The gang scattered, cursing.

'Run, you idiot!' Beanie tugged at Flint's arm. 'Come on! *Run!*' She ducked into the crowd.

Flint didn't need to be told three times. Following Beanie's red hat, he pushed his way into the milling shoppers. He barged, apologized, twisted, ran a few paces, twisted again. The mall was packed. It was difficult to get any speed up. As little Beanie cut through the crowd, like a fish through weeds, he bobbed and jerked to keep her in sight.

Shouts rang out around the mall. Men's voices – security guards barking directions at one another over the hubbub of shoppers and muzak. Flint glanced behind. Two men in uniform were pushing their way towards him. Neither old nor fat, they looked big and fiercely determined.

Beanie's red hat swerved towards the glass frontage of a large department store. Ducking low, Flint pushed towards the doors. The crowd thinned.

Inside, Beanie was scrambling onto an escalator. After the mall, the store seemed quiet and spacious, there was room to move. Flint sprinted.

'Stop them!' yelled a voice. 'Stop those kids!'

Flint didn't stop. Taking the first three steps at a leap, he scuttled, panting, past several startled shoppers. Beanie was disappearing off the top of the escalator. He turned to look back. The two men had now been joined by a third in a different uniform. 'You!' he barked. 'Wait there! That's an order.'

Flint froze.

The security guards scrambled past shoppers, onto the escalator. The frontrunner glared. 'Wait *there*! Hear me?'

But Flint had reached the top of the escalator. Beanie was beckoning by a display of saucepans. 'Come *on*! Move it!' Turning, she charged away past bewildered suited sales assistants. Flint took off in pursuit.

Past racks of saucepans and frying pans, past chip pans, pressure cookers, kettles, toasters and microwaves, Flint gained on Beanie. Glancing back, she took a sharp turn left behind a mountain of plastic food containers. Flint followed.

Beanie had spotted an escape route – she

was heading straight for an emergency exit: a *Push Bar To Open* sign. Flint accelerated to catch up.

Beanie crashed into the bar – and bounced back, straight into Flint. *'What!'* Grabbing the bar with both hands, she slammed it hard against the door, again and again, with all her weight.

Flint did the same. He felt the door shift, but only a few centimetres. Something was jamming it from the other side.

'I don't believe it!' Her face pure fury, Beanie gave the door a vicious kick. The emergency exit was locked.

'That's them!' The security guards charged into view, colliding with one another as they changed direction. The leader indicated for the other two to spread out. He looked angry and ugly. He looked like he was taking the chase *very* personally. 'All right, kids,' he grunted. 'The game's up.'

'Game?' mocked Beanie. 'If I'd known we were *playing* . . .' Suddenly, she was off again, running full tilt, close to the wall.

There wasn't time to think. Flint took off at her heels with the guards panting and shouting in pursuit. He and Beanie ran, turned, ran and turned again, past baffled, bemused and shocked shoppers. Every time they turned they left the guards further behind. *They were getting away.*

Suddenly, out of nowhere, a uniformed guard stepped from behind a display. He crouched low in Beanie's path, arms stretched wide like a goalie's. Nothing was coming past him. Beanie swerved and threw herself sideways.

Flint only felt the impact. He stumbled, ricocheted off a display and fell.

The air filled with an enormous crashing. Then silence.

A security guard lay beneath a toppled display rack; his colleagues stood staring, open-mouthed.

Flint staggered to his feet in a sea of shattered glass. *Where was Beanie?* He span round. She had vanished. *Scarpered.* He had to get away too. He ran.

And ran.

And halted.

'Leave *go!*' At the top of the down escalator, Beanie jerked and twisted in the arms of another security guard. She screamed as the large, mean-looking guard yanked back her arm, twisting it behind her back. 'Get *off* me!' she shrieked.

Charging like a rhino, Flint dropped his shoulder and threw himself.

The guard yelled, stumbled and tumbled.

The world went heavy and dark.

Speaking into the microphone on his lapel, grim-faced PC 397 read Flint's details from his notebook. A crackling radio voice read them back. PC 397 glanced at Flint. 'That all correct, is it, son?'

Flint nodded.

'No point lying,' the policeman warned. 'Computer'll tell us. You've enough on your plate already – thieving, criminal damage, assault.'

The other people in the room – the store manager, the security guards and a woman with several shopping bags, who it turned out was a plain-clothes store detective – stared grimly.

Flint looked at the floor. 'I never did anything.'

PC 397 frowned and tapped his ear. 'Come again?'

Flint scowled. 'I didn't do anything.'

'Didn't do anything . . . ?' PC 397 lent forward in his chair. Holding out his notebook, he pointed. 'Five minutes ago, you admitted to kicking Mr Malmholt on the shin. The poor chap was trying to apprehend a girl in the course of his duty!'

'She was screaming. He was hurting her.'

'And the young girl's name?'

Flint forced himself to meet the policeman's gaze. 'I told you, I only just met her. I only just met them. I don't know their names.'

'You hang around with a bunch of thieves and vandals. Some of them nick goods from a sports shop, another does several hundred pounds of damage to a cut-glass crystal-ware display . . .' PC 397 shook his head wearily, cynically. 'But you're telling me you don't know any of their names?'

Flint shrugged. Put like that it did sound farfetched, but he had to stick to his story. He wasn't about to grass.

'Today was the first time you met them?'

Flint nodded.

'But you've seen them around the place before?'

Flint nodded again.

'Where?'

Flint shrugged. Searching for the right lie. 'Just around. Streets and that. Mostly in the mall.'

PC 397's eyes narrowed. 'Trying to

protect their sort is a mug's game, son. They'll not thank you for it. We'll catch 'em. Always do. There's not an inch of this place isn't covered by closed circuit cameras. Their faces will all have been recorded.'

Flint nodded. 'Good.' He meant it. 'I'm innocent.' And that too. How would it look on the cameras? Would he come across as an accomplice? 'The cameras'll show you.' He pointed towards the other security guard. 'It was him that toppled the glass display.' He felt the guard's eyes, full of hatred. 'And while you're at it, you might want to try checking the first-floor emergency exits – they're locked. That can't be legal.'

The police radio crackled. *'Suspect's name and address confirmed. No previous. Over.'* PC 397 pressed a button. 'Message received. Over.' He glanced at Flint. 'Looks like you told us the truth – about that part at least.'

'Can I go now?'

PC 397's eyes flickered from the store manager back to Flint. He frowned. 'I'm going to be looking at the recordings from the cameras – in the sports shop, in the mall and here in the department store.

When I've done that, I'll be paying you a visit at . . .' he glanced at his notebook, '. . . Bella Gardens.'

Flint shrugged and nodded like – what did he care? But he *cared*. He was that worried he could barely keep from shaking.

The policeman's eyes narrowed. 'In the meantime, if you run into any of those nameless miscreants, you're going to call me at the station.' He leant forward, halitosis close. 'Do we understand one another?'

Flint nodded.

'Good. Now – clear off.'

CHAPTER 5
CLASH

Stretch ran with the ball. Dodging tackles, he charged forward zig-zagging in an amazing run. But for nothing – the opposition finally closed him down through weight of numbers and, when he ran out of space to run in, there was no-one in position for him to pass to.

Back in possession, the other team quickly moved the ball out to the wing. They had spotted a weakness. Stretch's players were gathered too closely, there was no-one covering the left flank. In seconds, opposition players had advanced up half the pitch and the ball was being pushed towards the goal. A sliding tackle from the defender in the red woollen hat halted the advance. The ball soared into touch.

Flint cupped his hands to his mouth. 'What's the score?'

Beanie stopped in her tracks. 'Hey! Where did *you* get to?'

Stretch whistled. 'Flint, you slacker! About time! We're getting crucified.'

The anger Flint had momentarily forgotten as he watched the game, came throbbing back. Where did he *get to*? *Slacker?* How *dare* they! But he forced it back down and, dumping his jacket, he ran on to the pitch.

Stretch and Beanie jogged over.

Flint glowered.

Beanie nodded sheepishly.

'Beanie's been defending like a terrier,' said Stretch, patting her on the back. He wiped sweat from his eyes. 'What's your left foot like?'

Flint shrugged. 'My right.'

'Excellent!' said Stretch. 'Now's your chance. Nidge is having to reinforce the centre. We need someone on the wing.'

Flint nodded. 'I noticed.'

'Time to find out what you're really made of, wonderboy.' Stretch pointed to where the throw-in was about to be taken.

'You're fresh. We expect your best.'

Fresh! Flint scowled. There was no time to explain what he'd been through. The ball was back in play. He sprinted to the far side. A boy he recognized from Stretch's team had gained hold of the ball and was looking to get rid of it. *'On the wing!'* yelled Flint. The ball came soaring. A well-judged pass. He trapped it. *'Get forward!'* He started a run.

Stretch and Nidge raced into the opposition half.

Flint slipped past a tackle, glanced across the field, passed and shifted into sprint mode.

Stretch nudged the ball down with his head, neatly bringing it under control with one touch. Dodging a tackle he chipped the ball over. *'Nidge!'*

Flint remembered Nidge from when he'd watched them play before. He was quick with his feet. Accelerating towards the goal, Nidge cut sharp left, skinning a couple of defenders on the way. Blocked by two more, he turned.

Thundering up the pitch, Flint signalled for the ball. The pass came straight to his feet – no need to slow or deviate. Locking sights on goal, he blasted.

The keeper leapt at full stretch, but never reached it.

Slumped exhausted in the shade of a horse-chestnut tree, the team sat or lay in dejected silence. Defeated.

Flint chewed at a stem of wild grass, watching the opposition saunter towards the distant park gates, mocking with their songs of victory. At the end of the match, Stretch had handed over money to the other side's captain – a prearranged bet on the outcome of the match. He hadn't said a word since. Nobody had.

Stretch stabbed the ground, again and again, with a short stick. 'Easy come, easy go.' he grunted. 'Least we never had to pay for the footballs.'

'Or the sports bag,' added Nidge. 'That must be worth a tenner at least.'

'Yeah!' Stretch grinned, pleased with himself. 'Yeah . . . we've come out on top, in spite of the stupid result.' The grin faded. He glanced at Flint. 'We could have won that match if we'd had eleven men.'

Flint held the gaze.

'Nice goal.' Stretch didn't blink. 'Shame you couldn't be here when we started.'

Nidge chuckled. 'Thought he was supposed to be the keen one.'

'Always the way . . .' Stretch looked around grinning. 'There's those that do . . . and those that talk about it.'

Laughter broke the group's tension.

Flint glared. 'You left out "those that mock".'

The laughter died.

'You make a joke out of everything,' growled Flint. 'Why d'you think I was so late?'

'Busy shopping?' Stretch chuckled. 'Beanie said she left you in a department store.'

'I got nicked.' Flint spat the words. 'Thanks to you.'

Sheepish eyes looked away. Heads bowed.

Stretch still grinned.

'It's *not* funny,' snapped Flint. 'I had to spend an hour being interrogated by a shop manager, a bunch of security guards and the law. About something I hadn't done. I wasn't laughing.'

'Beanie was worried about you,' said Stretch. 'Make any new friends?'

Meaning, did he grass? Flint searched

Stretch's face. 'What if I told you I gave them your name?'

Stretch stared back, dark pits. His arm returned to its mechanical rhythm, stabbing the stick into the ground.

'I barely know you,' snapped Flint, 'and you don't know me. But you took my silence for granted.' He caught Beanie's anxious glance. *Ease off! You're on dangerous ground. Don't provoke him.*

Stretch pressed down on the stick, forcing it deeper into the turf.

'I've got a family interested in me.' Flint fought to keep the tremble in his chest out of his voice. 'If I get charged, that's my chances ruined. The cop told me if I gave the names of the boys who stole the footballs, I'd be let off.'

'So what did you tell them?' Stretch's tone was flat.

'The truth,' said Flint. Let Stretch sweat. 'I said I didn't have anything to do with the theft . . .'

Stretch waited.

'I told them I didn't know the boys who had done the thieving . . .'

Stretch's eyes narrowed.

'And I couldn't give them any names.'

'That's all right then.' Stretch sneered.

Flint watched heads and eyes lift. They thought the storm was over. Snatching up a broken branch, he snapped it in two with a sharp *crack*. Faces twitched. *'No it isn't!'* Flint pointed at Stretch. 'It isn't all right! You *used* us. You and Nidge set us up to help you get away with your thieving.'

Stretch frowned.

'I've been wasting my time hanging out with you lot.' Scrambling to his feet, Flint looked around at the group. Beanie looked shocked. Nobody else wanted eye contact. 'You could have won that match this afternoon.' Flint hurled one of the pieces of stick out across the park. 'You could have, but you threw it away.'

'And your talent would have made all the difference?' Stretch smirked.

Flint shook his head. 'You didn't need me. You needed to give a damn. You didn't care.'

'Ah!' Stretch laughed. 'How sweet! He wants us to *care*.'

'You're losers!' Flint hurled the remaining piece of stick high out over the pitch. It fell to the ground on the far side. 'You're going nowhere,' he snapped. Scowling at Beanie, he turned and headed for the gates.

CHAPTER 6
NEWS

Flint shook his head.

'No names?' insisted Beanie. 'Nothing?'

'Nothing.' Flint snatched up the pillow and punched it angrily. 'What d'you take me for?'

Beanie looked awkward. 'No, that's good. It's just – the way you were carrying on yesterday, you didn't seem too happy about how things turned out . . .'

'Didn't seem too happy!?' Flint snorted. 'What do you expect! The two of us meet up with your *hardcore* mates for a game of football and I end up getting nicked . . . How am I supposed to feel?'

'Shhh.' Beanie put a finger to her lips. 'Keep your voice down.'

Flint punched the pillow hard. 'Course I'm not happy – I'm holding my breath! I get my first really good chance of being placed: I like Mr and Mrs Baker, they like me, the ball's rolling. Then *this* happens.'

'You never even did anything wrong.'

'Why you telling *me*?' Flint flung the pillow at the wall. 'I know that – I was there.'

Beanie stared at the floor. 'I'm sorry. I said how grateful I was. You'll be all right. They can't do you for something you didn't do.'

'Can't they!'

'If you hadn't come to help, it would've been me that got nicked.' Beanie glanced towards the door. Footsteps.

'*Flint?*' Sandra, outside on the landing. She sounded tense.

Flint scrambled to his feet.

A sharp rap. 'Flint, I need to talk to you.'

Flint opened the door.

Sandra's eyes scanned the room. 'Oh! You've got company.' She glanced towards Beanie. 'Sorry, love – Flint and I need a word in private.'

Beanie made a huffing sound.

With a gracious, wide-sweeping gesture of her hand, Sandra bowed and held open the door. 'It won't take long, princess. It's important.'

Beanie slid to her feet and shuffled reluctantly towards the landing.

'Make yourself a drink,' said Sandra. 'He's all yours when I'm finished.' She sighed and pushed the door closed. 'So . . .'

Flint took a deep breath. 'So . . . ?'

'I've just been discussing you.'

The police. Flint felt his heartbeat quicken. *So soon.* His chest tightened. PC 397 said he would be round.

'We need to set up another meeting.' Sandra sat on the chair. 'Mr Baker has suggested a visit to Welbeck YFC. How does that grab you?'

'Mr Baker? Welbeck!?' Flint somersaulted onto the bed. *'Fantastic!'*

Bushes rustled in the wind; trees rubbed, bark against bark, creaking and groaning. Flint was perched on the window ledge, but only silence crowded out from the empty house. He dropped into the dark room, held his breath and listened. *Nothing.*

Beanie had to be here. Her room had been empty. This was where she always came unless she was out wandering.

Something in her just wasn't comfortable with proper indoors. It made her jumpy, claustrophobic.

'Bean?' Flint called out from the bottom of the stairs. The house felt cold and still. 'Anyone there?' One step at a time, he crept upwards. Past the first hole and looking for the second, he paused – a sound coming from one of the upstairs rooms. A stifled sniffling sound. Or was it wind, howling through the empty windows? He kept climbing.

At first, the room appeared empty. But as Flint's eyes adjusted to the contrast of light and dark, he made out a figure curled up in the old armchair next to the window. 'Beanie?' He approached.

The figure turned, silhouetted against the gaping window.

'Beanie?'

She sniffed. 'Your new family want you, don't they?'

Flint moved round in front of her. 'You heard something then?'

Beanie nodded.

'It's early days yet,' said Flint. 'Too early to say.'

Beanie wiped her eyes and lowered her head.

Flint leant against the broken window frame. 'Jim – Mr Baker – coaches a football club.'

'A youth team?'

'Yeah – Welbeck.'

'That's nice.' Beanie managed a slight smile. 'You won't be so far away then. I used to live near there.' She sniffed and wiped her nose on her sleeve. 'Good reputation, Welbeck.'

'Yeah?'

Beanie nodded. 'Top division. Go back years.' She frowned. 'The area's changed though.'

'How d'you mean?'

Beanie tugged at the ripped upholstery. 'All been tarted up. The block we used to live in got pulled down. Council finally spent money. And now rich people are moving in.'

'It that bad?'

'You tell me.' Beanie shrugged. 'They make all those improvements, then locals can't afford to live there.' Her fingers jabbed and plucked at the armchair stuffing. 'The neighbourhood's been broken up.'

'Jim and Janet have lived there twenty years.' Flint felt defensive. 'Jim reckons he'll be able to get me a try-out with the club.'

'You're moving already?' Alarm.

'No.' Flint shook his head. 'That's a long way off. Sandra's just arranged for me to meet them down the club.'

Beanie sat up. 'This could be it – your try-out! Just what you need.'

Flint nodded. 'Jim wants me to bring my kit.' He crossed his fingers.

'That's brilliant!'

Flint felt Beanie's arms wrap around him. He hugged her back. 'Yeah. Good news for a change.'

CHAPTER 7
THE CLUB

'Looks like they're about to start playing,' said Sandra. 'I'll catch you up.'

'Thanks.' Flint slammed the car door and headed off.

Laughing and chatting, a group of boys in yellow and orange patterned shirts, orange shorts and striped socks, made their way over to the pitches.

'Hey!' yelled Flint. 'Where can I find the coach?'

A boy in the centre of the group looked Flint up and down. His slanted eyebrows lent him a sneering haughty look. 'The coach to where?' He pointed. 'Bus station's that way.' The others laughed.

Flint smiled good-naturedly. 'Jim Baker.'

'Today's training day. Coach'll be busy.' The boy turned his back dismissively. 'If you're looking for a trial, you should come back during the week and speak to the club secretary.'

'We have an *appointment*.' Sandra strode up alongside Flint. She meant business. 'With the coach, not the secretary.'

The boy looked her up and down the same way he had scrutinized Flint. He nodded towards a single-storey brick building. 'In there.' He turned to his teammates. 'Come on.'

Sandra and Flint watched the boys jog off towards the pitch. They, themselves, made their way towards the clubhouse.

'Aha!' Jim Baker's cheery face greeted them at the door. 'Good to see you both.' They shook hands. Jim flashed Flint a wink. 'We've at least a couple of boys off today. I could slot you in if you're interested.'

Flint nodded. 'Definitely.'

Sandra glanced at the darkening sky. 'Is there somewhere I can watch from indoors?'

'Of course.' Jim pushed the door open. 'Just up there on the left is the cafeteria.

Special day today — Janet's helping out behind the counter. Very rare.'

'Right. Have a good time.' Sandra grinned. 'See you later. I'll stay for a bit, but Jim's going to bring you home.'

'Come on, then.' Jim patted Flint's shoulder and nodded towards where the boys in orange and yellow were warming up. 'Let me present you to the squad.'

Some of the boys were passing balls to one another, keeping up a rhythm — trap, reposition, pass; trap reposition pass. Others were jogging, taking little spurts of sprinting to warm and stretch their muscles. A few were practising shots against the goalie.

'They're smart lads,' said Jim. 'Done very well so far this season. A couple are a bit inclined to sit back and take it easy.' He grinned. 'From what I've seen of your ball skills, your presence today might shake 'em up a bit.' He blew loudly on his whistle. '*Right!* Gather round.'

It had been a struggle. The other boys were all far more used to playing with one another and knew each other's names, skills and weaknesses. And of course they all knew his name because they only had one new name to learn. In the first session Jim had mixed first-team regulars with reserves and swapped players around every few minutes to give everybody some variety. Flint realized it was also so Jim could assess where he played best.

This first session had been fun. Rain had come in a sudden heavy downpour, soaking them in seconds and temporarily waterlogging the pitch, making it hard to do anything sensible. With strikers playing in goal and defenders playing up front, there had been some hilarious moments and nobody had felt they were under scrutiny or to blame if they got things wrong. As the new face, though, Flint had sensed the scrutiny, not just from Jim but every other boy on the pitch.

The wind that had dispersed the rain had also dried the pitch. In the second session, Flint found himself playing in a blue bib for the reserves. With everyone now in positions they were accustomed to, it became possible to see where the skills really lay and how disciplined the first team were.

Flint started on the right wing; demonstrating his pace and passing skills, he quickly set up one goal and scored another.

Reacting to this new danger, the first-team defenders adjusted their positions to close him down. Jim congratulated the defenders on their initiative and moved Flint to central midfield.

The first team were as strong in attack as defence. And as the reserves struggled to adjust to their new formation, Flint found himself playing an increasingly defensive role.

'Come on, we should be thrashing them!' The haughty-looking boy who had mocked and been so obstructive when Flint had earlier asked for directions, now captained the first team from the front. His name was Aldo. Passing the ball out to the left he ran forward.

Flint stayed with him. There had been no discussion among the reserves about who should mark who but, unless someone told him otherwise, he was making Aldo his responsibility.

Matthew, the first-team's gaunt winger, gained twenty yards before defenders began to harass. With calm precision he lofted a pass that sailed into the box.

The keeper watched the ball like a hawk. 'Where's my cover?' he yelled, charging out to fist the ball.

Aldo reached the cleared ball first.

But Flint's sliding tackle came a second later, blasting the ball clean away.

Aldo scowled.

'Don't just stand there!' The keeper waved big gloved hands at his defenders.

Two blue-bibbed boys rushed. But Matthew beat them to it and clipped the ball back into the box.

As Aldo jumped, Flint leapt beside him. The ball should have been his, but a sharp jab to his ribs caused him to twist away in pain. He fell clumsily to the ground, rolling to his feet in time to see the ball shake the net.

Aldo celebrated his third goal. His eyes challenged Flint. *Accuse me – I dare you!*

Swallowing pride, Flint turned away and jogged back to his half.

The whistle blew. The reserve forwards passed the ball out to the wing and began to advance. With renewed confidence following their goal, the first team harried and chased.

The reserves clung to possession with increasingly desperate passes.

'Come *on*,' yelled Jim. 'Let's see you moving forward.'

But it was hopeless. As fast as a reserve

player moved into a space, a first-teamer was there to mark him. It was two steps forward, three steps back. They were retreating all the time, back into their own half.

Aldo made a tackle. The ball rolled free.

Seizing the chance, Flint charged. With the ball at his feet and at last moving forward, he felt a surge of energy. He crossed the centre line sprinting.

'Don't just stand there!' Aldo's furious yell echoed across the pitch. 'Block him off!'

Flint raced on, first-team players closing on him from three different angles. From the corner of his eye he glimpsed blue on the wing. He passed, vaulted a late high tackle, and kept running.

The boy on the wing was in the clear. Stretching his legs, he flew towards the goal line, first team players chasing in his wake.

Thundering towards the goal, Flint raised a hand and yelled, *'Pass!'*

The ball soared in.

Flint dived.

The net shook.

'Played!'

As Flint got to his feet, Jim blew two

short blasts on his whistle. 'Excellent.' He threw Flint a wink. 'OK, lads. We have to cut it short there. I've been summoned.' He gestured towards the clubhouse. 'Good effort. Three times round the field, then in and get changed.'

CHAPTER 8
THE COMMITTEE

In the changing rooms, Flint had felt like an outsider. Of course that's what he was – he was new, it was his first day and he couldn't have expected any different. But there was something about Aldo and the way the other boys looked up to him that made Flint uneasy. Aldo seemed to resent his presence at the club.

Only a couple of the boys had kept themselves to themselves and not joined in with Aldo's snide remarks. Not that any of it had bothered Flint unduly. He was smart enough to know that if you didn't show a sense of humour about yourself, you would be mercilessly and relentlessly mocked. So he had smiled, shrugged and laughed it off.

But there was little temptation to hang about. As soon as he had changed, he had nodded goodbye, shouldered his kit-bag and made his way through to the clubhouse.

Welbeck was a big club, catering for all ages. Wandering through the building amongst fresh-out-of-the-shower players and their parents, Flint was pleased to spot a familiar face.

With her tight-lipped smile, Janet beckoned him over to where she was serving behind the cafeteria counter. 'Jim's in a meeting with the management. The rest of them will all have had their tea and biscuits. Would you mind taking a cuppa through for him? Grab yourself something first.'

'Good idea.' Flint eyed the plates of biscuits, chocolate bars and cakes greedily. 'I'm starving after all that running about.'

'What would you like?' Janet followed his gaze. 'No – let me guess . . .' She reached for the plate of chocolate cake.

Flint nodded and rummaged in his pockets for money.

'Don't worry about that.' Janet wagged a finger. 'Compliments of the club.' As she passed him the large slice of cake wrapped in a paper napkin, she leant forward. 'Not a word to anyone,' she whispered, 'or I'll be had up before the committee.'

With Jim's tea in one hand, and the chocolate cake in the other, Flint followed Janet's directions, scoffing as he went. Lost in chocolate heaven, he made a wrong turning and ended up by the bins outside the back. But finally, at the end of the corridor, where Janet had described it, he found the door with the sign: MANAGEMENT COMMITTEE.

Flint hesitated. Voices were being raised on the other side of the door. It was difficult to make out the words, but it was clear strong opinions were being expressed inside the room. A man was shouting; Jim was shouting back.

Devouring the last morsel of cake, Flint wiped his mouth and knocked. The angry to and fro of voices abruptly halted. The door opened.

A long table stretched the length of the room. Seated around it, Flint counted ten men and two women. At the nearest side of the table next to a younger man in a tracksuit, Jim looked flushed. The younger man had plenty of hair but a pinched, rather weasely-looking face.

Rising from his seat, Jim smiled and beckoned. 'This is Flint.' He turned to the suited man at the head of the table. 'The boy I mentioned.'

'Blanchard.' The suited man nodded stiffly. 'Pleased to meet you.' His restless fingers fiddled with a pen.

With the attention of every person in the room focused on him, Flint felt horribly self-conscious. He handed Jim his cup of tea.

Jim winked. 'Thanks, Flint. Thank Janet for me.'

'I'll see you later then.'

Back in the empty corridor, Flint pressed his ear to the door and listened. It was Blanchard who had been shouting. There had been an uneasy tension between him and Jim – over what?

Hurrying back up the corridor, Flint nipped out the back past the bins and round the rear of the building. As he crouched by the window of the management committee room, on the other side of the glass Blanchard glanced around the table. 'I'd like it if we reached some kind of sensible conclusion. There are still other matters I want to discuss.' Blanchard's stare came to rest on Jim.

'I haven't had time to read all the accounts,' said Jim. 'What I do know is if we raise subs again we make it harder for talent with no money to join.'

Blanchard glanced at the smartly dressed woman seated beside him. 'Margaret?'

'The treasurer's report makes it perfectly clear that if we wish to follow the plans for expansion as agreed at last year's AGM, we simply have to generate more revenue.' The woman glanced around the table.

With degrees of enthusiasm, the committee nodded their assent.

The woman addressed herself to Jim. 'Your objection might be valid if we didn't have a waiting list of boys all dying to join the club. To cater for demand, we need to expand. We'll have no problem filling places at the new rate of sub.'

'The club's worked wonders over the years,' said Jim, 'and built a reputation second to none.' The proud smile faded. 'By upping the sub and restricting ourselves to boys from well-off families, we're kissing that reputation goodbye.'

Committee members shifted uncomfortably in their seats.

'Talent.' Jim's eyes sparkled. 'Raw talent is the lifeblood of every club. Without it, the club will die.'

Blanchard applauded. 'Noble sentiments which I'm sure all of us would echo. However, if the fees are too high, tell me how come we're still managing to top the leagues?' He chuckled. 'The good results continue. Are we to understand that is purely down to your skills as coach?'

'Of course not.' Jim scowled at the faces round the table. 'But how many here are local people? We've been importing our talent.'

'And parents of talented boys', said Blanchard, 'will continue to bring their sons here at the rate of sub we propose to charge. They come from far and wide, because we have established and *maintain* an excellent reputation.'

Jim grunted. 'What about the good players we're not even seeing because they can't pay the rate?'

Flint thought of Stretch and the others he had played with. They were lazy, totally disorganized and lacking any motivation, but there was no doubting their talent. Perhaps they had good reason to be cynical.

'Surely,' continued Jim, 'Welbeck's priority should be bringing local talent into their game, not maximizing income.'

'But we have to be realistic, Mr Baker.' The smartly dressed woman leant forward. 'At the end of the day we have to balance the books.'

Jim glowered. 'This is a football club.' His fists clenched. 'But since you and your associates took over the management committee you have been running it for profit and as a social club for your cronies. Do you want my frank opinion?'

Blanchard smiled sourly. 'Isn't that what you've been giving us?'

'You,' said Jim, pointing, 'and your little friends are out to turn Welbeck into an elitist, exclusive institution. You don't care about football. This club would be better off without you.'

Blanchard's face showed no emotion. 'Mr Baker, if we could have passed this motion earlier we might by now have moved on to the other matters in hand and you would have learned that next week I plan to launch a tournament for local clubs, funded entirely by my business.'

Around the table, raised eyebrows, nods and murmurs of approval suggested surprise at this proposal. Only Jim was frowning.

'There will be a cup,' continued Mr Blanchard. 'The Blanchard Trophy – to be awarded annually to the winners. The competition will be played following the final week of our league season.'

Jim glanced around the table at the enthusiastic faces.

'The tournament will be open to all-comers regardless of standard, facilities, et cetera. And of course there will be a generous prize for the winning team.' Blanchard smiled. 'Does that please you?'

Jim shook his head. 'You couldn't have picked a worse time for it. The end of a hard season. That's when the boys should be taking it easy. They won't have had time to recover.'

'You're carping, Mr Baker. It's just one more day. There will still be plenty of time for them to rest afterwards.'

'Presumably there's an entry fee?' Jim scowled. 'Sounds to me like you're getting other no-hope teams to pay for a trophy which your own team have the best chance of winning.'

'OK. You've had your little say.' Blanchard was beginning to sound irritable. 'Enough's enough. It's time we took a vote.' His eyes darted round the table. The committee members nodded their agreement. 'Those in favour of the motion to raise club subs in line with the proposal, raise their hands.'

Flint counted.

Shifting uncomfortably in his seat, the tracksuited man sitting next to Jim sheepishly raised his hand.

'I make that ten,' said the woman taking notes by the door.

'Those against?'

Jim's hand was alone.

Blanchard beamed triumphantly. 'Motion carried.'

'Shameful decision.' Jim shook his head. 'Won't do you any good either. Without a unanimous decision it won't get passed at the AGM. And you can rest assured – I'll not be swayed.'

'We'll see.' Blanchard smiled sourly. 'A lot can happen between now and then.'

CHAPTER 9
TROUBLE

A police car pulled up. Flint's heart skipped a beat. Instinctively he slid from the windowsill and crouched out of sight.

He listened.

The engine cut. Doors clunked.

Cautiously he raised himself, just high enough to peer into the street. Two officers, a man and a woman, were crossing the road towards Bella Gardens. They paused in front of the building and looked up. *PC 397!* Flint ducked back below the sill. *This was it. They had come for him!*

A rap on the door made him jump. Beanie burst in. 'Oh!' She stopped in her tracks. 'You've seen, then?'

Flint nodded.

Beanie dropped to the floor beside him. 'You recognized them?'

Flint nodded again. 'The man.'

'What are you going to say?'

Before Flint could reply, there was another knock at the door.

'Well?' Sandra prickled. 'You've heard the officer's report – what have you got to say for yourself?'

Flint stared sheepishly at the carpet. 'It wasn't my fault. I didn't know them. I had no idea what they were planning.'

'And this girl that you were with . . .'

Flint's heart raced.

Sandra turned to PC 397. 'Did you get a look at her on the video tapes?'

PC 397 nodded.

'She wasn't, by any chance, rather slight? Wearing a red woollen hat?'

PC 397 smiled wryly. 'Sounds like you know her.'

Sandra nodded. 'No point in looking for her now though; she's bound to have made herself scarce.' She scowled. 'So what has to happen?'

'Well . . .' PC 397 straightened his back. 'Whenever a minor has dealings with the police, we're obliged by law to notify their parents or guardians.'

Flint felt his breath shudder.

PC 397 looked over towards him. 'In this particular case we're satisfied the young lad here has told us the truth. Seems pretty clear from the CCTV footage he wasn't one of the perpetrators. He claims he got caught up in the chase involuntarily – out of panic. The tapes appear to substantiate that.'

Flint bit his lip and forced himself to meet the policeman's gaze.

Sandra frowned. 'What about the incident involving all that broken glass in the department store?'

'Ah . . .' PC 397 nodded. 'Fortunately for young Flint here, the store's own CCTV footage bears out his story. The owner of the business has decided not to press charges.'

Sandra leaned forward. 'Who will foot the bill?'

'Mr Blanchard's insurance company, I imagine.'

Flint gave a start. 'Mr *Blanchard*?'

The adults turned.

Flint wanted to vanish in a puff of smoke. 'Odd-sounding name!'

PC 397's eyes narrowed suspiciously. 'Not for the owner of Blanchard's Department Store, it isn't.'

CHAPTER 10
NEW LIFE

Flint made his way down the corridor and into the changing room. Slinging his kitbag on the bench, he slumped down beside it and let his eyes wander round the empty space.

In such a short time his world had changed completely. Officially fostered. Officially a member of Welbeck YFC. Officially no criminal record. Things had turned out all right. He was living in a proper home at last – a real lived-in house, a place that didn't smell of lino and cheap carpet, somewhere that wasn't kitted out in plastic stacking chairs and ugly easy-clean sofas. Now, finally, his world had a personal quality; his new home had warmth and character.

Janet and Jim had made him feel welcome and cared for. Even before he had moved in with them his evenings and weekends had increasingly been spent at the club, watching to begin with, then when everything had been sorted, training with the squad. It felt like he had known Jim all his life. Janet was more reserved. But, living under the same roof, little by little, he and Janet were getting to know each other too.

Weeks had flown past. And now, just a couple of months after his first visit to the club, here he was – finally picked for the team, about to play his debut: a big match against Welbeck's toughest rivals, Broadmarsh. Jim had kept off picking him for a while, wary some of the boys or their parents might think he was giving Flint special treatment or allowing him to queue-jump. But with one midfielder dropped out injured and another off sick, Jim'd had no choice but to use him.

He had *arrived*.

There'd been other changes. He'd been back to Bella Gardens a couple of times, but he had given up on Stretch and his pack of losers a long time ago. It'd been a while since he'd seen Beanie too. As well as Jim, Janet and the football club, he had new clothes, new trainers and spending money. He'd even been to visit the local school he'd be joining. There was a lot about this new life to feel good about.

But along the way, something else seemed to have changed. Ever so subtly Jim's mood and manner had altered. Before, there had always been a sparkle about him, an enthusiasm and good humour; he had always been ready with a joke or witty comment, his energy and optimism had shone forth. But now the wisecracks had dried up, and though he still put on a smile, still talked the talk of a good coach, he wasn't the same. It was as if something had *died* in him.

To begin with Flint had worried that the change was somehow his doing – that it had something to do with his moving in and Jim becoming his official foster father. But increasingly he suspected Jim's alteration had to do with Blanchard and the business about the club's subs.

Voices and footsteps echoed in the corridor. The changing-room door swung open. Blanchard entered, behind him Aldo and Jim. 'Hey!' Blanchard beamed as he strode over. 'Our newest signing.' He grasped Flint's hand and shook it warmly. 'Good to have you on board.'

Uncomfortable with his father's display of enthusiasm, Aldo pretended to check the contents of his sports bag.

Blanchard patted Flint on the back. 'Jim's foster son! Quite a player, I gather. When he told us it was in the pipeline, we were delighted – isn't that right, Jim?'

'Certainly,' Jim smiled. 'Flint'll be an asset.'

Blanchard laughed heartily. 'This match against Broadmarsh promises to be a tough one. Looking forward to seeing you in action at last.'

Flint punched the air and ran over to where the supporters cheered and applauded in front of the clubhouse. It had been a beautiful goal: great set-up and strike, followed by a rebound; then the perfectly timed finish. His second goal of the match.

For an opening contribution there could hardly have been a better start. Two goals! As Flint made his way back towards Welbeck's half, teammates ran over to pat him on the back and congratulate.

Aldo came to pay his respects. 'Great goal.' His sour expression belied his words. 'But how about sticking to your job. Leave the goal-scoring to the forwards.'

Flint scowled. By *the forwards* Aldo meant *Aldo*. He had been pushing the same line at every practice. It was getting tiresome. 'A rebound,' snapped Flint. 'No-one else near the ball. What was I supposed to do – *leave* it?'

Aldo tapped his captain's armband, turned and walked away.

Flint kicked at the turf. He had never been one of those players who just wanted to concentrate on one position and keep to that role. In most teams, unfortunately, that was what was required. After trying him out pretty much right across the field, Jim had decided to make him an attacking midfielder. Scoring was part of the job. Aldo's comments were out of order.

Flint's second had been Welbeck's fourth. Aldo had scored the other two. All four goals had been the result of good collective effort. But Flint sensed Aldo deeply resented the fact that someone else was scoring goals.

The opposition were tough and showed

no sign of surrender. Every time Welbeck scored, Broadmarsh soaked up the setback and returned to the game determined to answer with a goal of their own. Broadmarsh had opened the scoring and now, once again, the two sides were even.

'Go on, the Martians!' The Broadmarsh supporters, a motley group of mums, dads, brothers, sisters and family dogs, passionately urged their team on to victory.

More numerous and altogether better groomed, the Welbeck supporters countered with their own loud demands. 'Come on, Welbeck! One more goal!'

Flint recognized many of the faces he'd seen sitting round the table at the committee meeting – parents, he presumed. And Llewellyn, the tracksuited man who'd sat next to Jim, now stood beside him. Assistant coach, he trained some of the younger kids and occasionally turned up at first-team practices so Jim could give him coaching tips.

Broadmarsh, in their all-green strip, took their kick quickly and attacked once more.

'Keep your heads,' Aldo reminded his team. 'Tackle early.'

Flint and his fellow midfielders harried

relentlessly. Passing their way out of danger, the greens kept pushing forward. But this time a moment's hesitation gave the ball away.

Without a pause Jake, the right-back, lofted the ball. Suddenly Welbeck were back on the attack. Aldo and the forwards charged. The greens fell back in disarray.

Flint sprinted, determined to be right up with the action. But Aldo took a shot from way out. A defender lunged and the deflected ball flew out for a corner.

'A good ball wasted, Aldo.' Jim cupped hands to mouth. 'You're part of a *team*, remember.'

Aldo scowled and spat at the ground.

'Get back!' yelled the Broadmarsh coach from the touchline.

'Come on!' barked Broadmarsh's captain. 'Mark up!'

Flint held back, staying well out of the area, ready for stray balls or a sudden break from the defending team.

The corner came long and high. Too high. Boys jumped one after another, but no-one could get a head to it. Flint chased the ball, but Matt the winger was already on the case. Within seconds he was surrounded. Twisting and shoving he chipped the ball to Flint.

Broadmarsh were marking tightly in the box. Green shirts rushed out to block. Swerving round them, Flint cut towards the centre, took aim and blasted.

'Goal!'

'Beauty!' roared Jim.

He should have guessed there was going to be trouble. Everyone knew how jealously Aldo guarded his top-goal-scorer status. Aldo was always uncomfortable when others scored – but scoring more than him in your first proper match for the club? Flint had gone too far.

All of a sudden no-one wanted to pass to him. They hesitated. They threw away good opportunities. But all Jim's yelling from the touchlines didn't make a blind bit of difference. It was as if Aldo had sent out some discreet signal.

Stern words from Jim at half-time had made little difference either. The second half looked like continuing where the first half left off.

Aldo bungled a pass to a fellow forward. Flint had been the obvious choice for the pass. But now Broadmarsh had possession yet again. A goal behind, Welbeck couldn't afford to give away another.

Furious, Flint charged in for the tackle. The Broadmarsh forward swerved, and twisted, but Flint moved faster and stole the ball. Green shirts swarmed. Accelerating out of danger he looked round for support. To right and left there was no-one, but ahead of him three Welbeck players were running forward and had broken free of their markers. Aldo was one of them. Flint passed the ball out to the left.

'Get back, get back!' yelled the frantic Broadmarsh coach.

Now Flint was hurtling towards the box and the ball was coming back to him from Matt. He dodged the tackles, cutting a zig-zag path straight for the goal. Two Broadmarsh defenders eyed him warily. He ran at them, lofted the ball and barged his way through to collect.

'Go on!' roared Jim from the touchline. 'Nice one! Go *on*!'

'Take a shot!' yelled someone's mum.

Swerving round another defender, Flint charged towards the goal. Out of the corner of his eye, he caught a flash of Welbeck strip running beside him. Broadmarsh's keeper was coming out, arms stretched wide.

Suddenly Flint felt the Welbeck players press against him, *trying to edge him off the ball*.

'This one's mine!' Barging Flint out of the way, Aldo hooked the ball, chipped it round the keeper, and shot.

The whistle blew.

As the Welbeck supporters cheered and shouted, Aldo clenched his hands above his head, triumphant.

Grabbing Aldo's shirt, Flint wrenched him round, boiling with rage. 'Who do you think you are!?'

Aldo scowled. 'What are you talking about?'

Flint heard the referee's whistle, but he couldn't stop. He shoved Aldo hard. 'You *stole* that ball.'

'Stole?' Aldo shoved Flint back. 'It's a team game, remember?'

Flint sensed others gathering, he felt hands placating, restraining. But he was too angry to take heed. He shoved Aldo again. 'You barged me.'

'Don't be ridiculous!'

Flint shoved again, this time even harder. *'Deliberately.'*

Aldo scowled. 'You stumbled.'

Quite a crowd was gathering – players, referee, coaches and parents.

'Stop this at once!' Jim struggled to push his way through. 'Flint!'

Flint jabbed Aldo in the chest, raised a threatening fist, then shoved him again. 'You *barged*!'

'You tripped!' Aldo looked around, appealing to the gathered faces for support. 'He stumbled.'

'That's quite enough!' Red-faced and furious, Jim stepped between the two players.

The referee stood beside him. 'This stops NOW!' His furious eyes darted back and forth from Flint to Aldo. 'Would someone mind telling me what is going on?'

'I can't believe it!' Jim glowered. 'What kind of way is this to behave on pitch?'

Aldo sneered. Flint stared sullenly at the ground.

'I'm talking to both of you,' snapped Jim. Shaking his head he turned to the referee. 'From where I was standing, there seemed to be some very unconventional play from this one.' With a nod he indicated Aldo.

'Hey?' Aldo protested. 'Me!? I never!'

The referee silenced Aldo with a glare.

'I'm afraid my view was obstructed.' He turned to Flint. 'But there can be no place in this game for violent or aggressive behaviour.' He pointed towards the touchline. 'I'm sending you off.'

'What!' Flint felt rage boiling up inside. 'But you can't!'

'*Flint!*' Jim grabbed his arm, the grip was tight. 'You've had a good game.' He leant close, whispering. 'You've made one silly mistake. Don't make another.'

Flint scowled.

'Come on.' Jim tugged him out of the huddle. 'It's your first game. Don't mess things up for yourself.'

With only ten men, Welbeck lost. Watching the whole sorry slide into defeat from the touchline, it was hard to know what to feel. Flint was still furious that he'd been so unfairly removed from the game. But it felt like some kind of justice that, without his contribution, Welbeck were beaten.

Observing the team from the outside for the first time, Flint saw more clearly than ever just how much Aldo was only interested in one thing – Aldo scoring goals. Again and again Jim reacted to

Aldo's short-sighted selfishness. Flint sensed the growing frustration. Right up to the game's dismal end, Jim kept trying to redirect Aldo's play. But Aldo wasn't listening.

When the final whistle had blown, Aldo wasted no time making it clear who he blamed for Welbeck's defeat. 'Great debut, Flint!' he sniped, as the dejected team trudged off the pitch. 'Your contribution was really appreciated.' His words dripped sarcasm. 'First defeat of the season. Couldn't have done it without you.'

Flint's fists were clenched. He bit his lip.

'That's enough!' Jim stepped forward, glaring at Aldo. 'I want no more of that talk. It's *not* the captain's responsibility to point the finger.'

'No, of course,' Aldo sneered. 'That's our coach's job.' He turned to his teammates. 'And we all know who *he* won't blame . . .'

Jim opened his mouth to speak, but seemed to think better of it. The players were already moving off towards their waiting parents. Blanchard was there, stony-faced, watching. Shaking his head Jim patted Flint on the shoulder. 'Come on, son. Let's go home.'

Flint turned and followed. Not one boy had spoken out against Aldo's verdict. Not one player had even come over and told him they felt differently. So much for team spirit.

CHAPTER 11
NIGHT

Clambering out of his bedroom window in the dead of night – what was he thinking?

Flint stared down into the darkness. A ten-metre drop: and the choice of stone slabs or sharp spearhead-topped railings to fall on. *Ouch!* He closed his eyes and listened. Distant traffic on the high street. A phone ringing. Laughter. From somewhere behind him, the murmur of television voices downstairs in the house. Apart from that, the night was still; the neighbourhood was quiet.

What was it? Restlessness? Frustration? Loneliness? The new life not quite working out the way he'd hoped? All of these and pent-up rage about Aldo and Welbeck to boot. He just had to get out for a few hours. The same caged feeling he'd felt in the children's home was still there. He needed someone to talk to. Beanie would understand.

Flint reached out to grasp the drainpipe. The sturdy old metal sort, it felt cold under his fingers. He had checked it out in the daylight. It went straight down the wall past the landing window, linked up with a second pipe, then cut at forty-five degrees over the front room bay, across to a drainage grate at the corner of the house. Some kind of creeper ran up beside it.

Taking a long deep breath, Flint shuffled to the edge of the sill and swung out. The drainpipe gave a shudder as he clamped it with his legs. Alternating grip between feet and hands, he began his descent in the chill night air.

He had not descended two metres when the drainpipe lurched: the movement was small but sudden. He froze. From down below, ominous grating, grinding noises vibrated up the pipe – mortar and brick surrendering their hold on rusted bolts. He shuddered and the drainpipe shifted again.

A touch of panic. Below him, eager to impale, railings thrust upwards with their spike-tips. Flint stretched his foot against the brickwork, probing for support. *Nothing* . . . The foot flailed. *Nothing . . . nothing . . .*

Then, at last, something hard under foot. A flat-edged protrusion. A window ledge. *It had to be.* With most of his weight still precariously draped round the shaky tilted pipe, he needed a hand-grip, some means to haul himself to safety. His fingers groped blindly in the dark, inching across the brickwork.

At a place where mortar had eroded between the bricks, Flint dug and rubbed with his fingers, loosening the grains and forcing cement to crumble further. But with a sudden guttural rumble, the weary drainpipe lurched once more. *Too late!* Wedging fingers into the crack, he forced them to take the strain. It *hurt*. To hold it for more than a few seconds would be agony. One last breath, then, pressed close to the wall, he tightened muscles and swung.

The drainpipe shuddered and grunted. Fingers wrenched free. He clutched at the ledge, but it was too late. He was falling . . .

* * *

'Ouch!' Sucking air sharply through his teeth, Flint dabbed at the cut with a tissue. It stung! In the street lamp's glow he examined his grazes: a hand, an elbow and a shoulder. The left wrist felt sprained too. How was he going to explain that little lot? Assuming of course his crashing descent through the creeper hadn't already alerted Janet and Jim to his absence. And then there was the matter of the skewed drainpipe . . .

Jogging his way up the street, Flint picked out the dark silhouette of the derelict house. Though other houses in the street still had lights behind their curtains, the big black shape looked dead and empty. But it wouldn't be. Not on a Saturday night.

He'd been unlucky with the drainpipe, but he was still in one piece. He could still run, jump and kick. That was the main thing.

Making his way to the hole in the fence, Flint pushed aside a loose plank and stepped into the darkness.

* * *

88

'Look who it is!' Stretch's dark skin glowed in the firelight. His eyes glittered. 'Mr Keen.'

'I can tell you've missed me.' Scanning the shadows, Flint spotted familiar faces. Beanie's was one of them.

'So how's the football?' Stretch grinned. 'Been approached by any talent scouts?'

'Not yet.'

'Picked up by one of the big clubs?'

Flint smiled back. Never show a mocker that you care. He laughed. 'Nope. No-one's offered the right price.' And don't take yourself seriously. 'To be honest, I don't think anyone can afford me.'

Laughter from the shadows.

Beanie got to her feet and came over. 'How you getting on?'

'At home you mean?'

Beanie nodded. 'And the football.'

'Home is great,' said Flint. Maybe a touch more enthusiasm. 'Welbeck too. Top of the local league. I'm already playing matches *and* scoring goals for them.' Heads turned. He knew they were interested. Some of them, maybe even most, would've liked to have been in his shoes.

'Come to gloat?' Stretch sneered. 'Glad it's all working out so nicely for you.'

'Course you are.' Flint watched the eyes in the room flicker from him to Stretch and back again. Stretch tried to hide his envy behind sarcasm. They couldn't see it. 'You'd swap places with me right now,' said Flint, 'if you weren't so scared of what this lot think. You're worried you'll lose respect if they discover you really want the same as everyone else.'

'Yeah, yeah, yeah.' Stretch laughed. 'Like living with a sad old couple and joining some jumped-up football clubs where mummies and daddies all come along to cheer.'

'You want to be careful,' said Flint. 'Carrying such a big chip on your shoulder you might put your back out. I'm not like you, Stretch, I want to *do* things. I want *a life*.'

Stretch shook his head. 'It don't work like that. You'll always be an outsider in that club, in that neighbourhood. Be wary. Watch your back.' The leer. 'Don't be fooled – your so-called teammates'll never really accept you.'

'Sour grapes,' Flint scoffed. 'What do you know!' But Stretch's words had jangled his nerves. He felt defensive. 'You hate the fact I'm making it work.'

'Yeah, I'm all cut up about it.'

'You have to believe something poisonous will spoil it all, because you're going nowhere. Doing nothing.'

Stretch's face changed. Getting to his feet, he looked mean and deadly. 'You live in a fantasy world, kid.' He jabbed Flint in the chest. 'You think your new parents are going to accept you like you were their own?'

'Why not?'

'And your new club will put you in the first team I suppose?'

'They already have.'

Stretch snorted.

'You have to *want* something,' said Flint. 'Things don't just happen – you have to make them happen. You don't get it, do you? Am I the best footballer here?'

'*No!*' The answer from the room was resounding.

'Exactly!' Flint smiled. 'But I'm training with a club and I've played my first match. I'm going to be playing matches every week. You could be too. All of you. Except you've given up before you've even started.'

Stretch shook his head. 'You think you're better than us.' His eyes pierced. 'You think you can become one of them. But be warned, sonny boy . . .' He jabbed Flint again. 'You're going to wake up with a bump.'

CHAPTER 12
INTERROGATION

Flint took a sip of tea – it was cold. He had slept badly and when Janet had brought him his early morning cuppa it'd been a struggle to open his eyes. She'd seemed tense – not brittle, or brusque like she could be sometimes, more *concerned*. He had fallen back asleep. Now he was late for breakfast.

Buttoning up his jeans, Flint reached across the bed for a T-shirt. Small rust-coloured blobs, conspicuous on the clean white sheets, caught his eye. *Blood.*

Last night! Instinctive fingers searched out the underside of his elbow: a sticky scab was forming. Tender. He probed the grazed shoulder, squeezed the stiff wrist.

The fall came flashing back, blow by blow. He must have been crazy – what had he been thinking? He had gone looking for Beanie, needing to talk to someone who knew him. Instead he'd ended up arguing with Stretch. Again.

Discarding the T-shirt, Flint turned to the wardrobe in search of something with sleeves that would cover his elbow. Stretch's words had been rattling round his head all night.

Pulling on a sweatshirt, he looked around for his trainers. Stretch had been right about him being an outsider. He'd always been one though. He could handle that. That was nothing new.

But what about the good feelings he'd had about Jim and Janet. And what if the hopes he'd had about the club and football had all been wrong? Maybe the clash with Aldo was just the start, the thin end of the wedge . . .

Stretch's negativity was getting to him.

Tugging the duvet up to cover the sheets, Flint shook the stiffness from his limbs. Tired and aching was bad enough, but *cranky* was never a good way to start a day.

* * *

'Freshly squeezed.' Janet handed Flint a glass of orange.

'Thanks.' Something was up. He knew it by the way she looked at him. There was atmosphere.

'Jim's popped down to the shops.'

Flint reached for the cereal packet.

Janet's hand was there first. 'I'd like to talk about last night.'

'Last night?'

Janet nodded.

'OK.' Flint shrugged awkwardly. The cereal box was pushed towards him.

'Apparently you went out.'

Guilty. Flint stiffened. Hurt was visible in Janet's face. Betrayed trust. He poured cereal into the bowl. 'Yeah.' Nonchalant.

'Jim and I were in the front room. We never saw you leave.'

But they must have heard him return. Creeping silently up those stairs in the dark had been impossible. Flint lowered his eyes. 'It was late. I knew you wouldn't want me out at that time...' He took a gulp of orange.

Janet watched. She wanted to know how he had done it – how he had left the house undetected.

Another gulp. And another. Flint

finished the juice and wiped his mouth. Janet was still waiting. He took a deep breath. 'I climbed down from my window.'

'From your *bedroom*!' Janet's face fell. 'The top of the house!' She stared horrified.

Flint's mouth dried. Janet appeared frail all of a sudden. *Shaken*. 'Sorry.'

'I don't know what to say.' Janet bit her lip. 'You're safe at least. I suppose we should be thankful.' She straightened her back. 'So . . . where did you get to?'

Flint poured milk over the cereal – slowly, thoroughly, hoping an inspired way of avoiding the truth might spring to mind. He stirred with his spoon. 'I met up with some mates.' He took a mouthful, munched, smiled – as though going out with mates was what he always did on a Saturday night.

'Boys your age?' Perturbed.

Flint shrugged. What would worry her least? 'I'm younger than most of them – I think.'

'And where do you all meet?'

Flint hesitated. 'Perhaps I should have just asked?' He took another spoonful. 'You and Jim might not have minded.'

'What kind of place?' Janet wasn't going to be side-tracked.

Flint tried to make the mouthful last. 'Someone's house.'

Janet sensed withheld information. Her eyes narrowed. 'Whose?'

Flint shrugged. 'Dunno. It's empty.'

'*Empty?*' Janet frowned.

'Derelict.'

The frown deepened.

'There's a gap in the fence,' said Flint. 'The garden's overgrown, practically jungle. The ground-floor windows are missing. It's easy to get in.' He took another mouthful. 'Probably waiting to be demolished.'

Janet sighed uneasily. 'A place like that ought to be better secured.' She shivered. 'It sounds dangerous.'

Recalling the fall, Flint stirred his cereal and tried to swallow.

Janet reached across the table and took Flint's hand. 'I don't approve of what you did, but at least you've had the decency to be honest.' She squeezed. 'Promise me, please, you won't do that again.'

Flint nodded.

'Thank you.' Tired smile.

'It's not like me,' said Flint. 'I just felt . . .' The words were slipping out. 'I needed to see someone.'

'Perhaps you're feeling a bit isolated?'

Flint nodded again.

'And disappointed?' Janet's hand squeezed again, gently. Her face had softened. 'All that business on the pitch? Jim told me about it.'

'Getting sent off,' said Flint. 'It just got to me.'

From the hall came the sound of the front door closing.

Janet fiddled with the edge of the tablecloth. 'I sent Jim to get something for his indigestion. I thought it might be better if I had a word with you alone.' She glanced anxiously towards the hall. 'He's got a lot on his mind at the moment. I didn't want to add to his worries.'

Watching Janet pick at crumbs, Flint realized suddenly that he and his reckless night-time antics had not been the only reason for her looking so worried. Not even the main reason. Something was troubling her. Something about Jim. Troubling her badly.

'Here's an opportunity all you up-and-coming young footballers – boys and girls – won't want to miss . . .'

Flint reached over and turned up the volume.

'Sudden Death In July – a brand new football competition open to all-comers,' intoned the radio DJ, *'sponsored by Blanchard's, our local department store.'*

Jim glared at the stereo. The car's gears made a horrible grinding sound as he changed down to take the corner.

'This is a knockout competition with a difference, folks. All the matches are going to be played on a single day.'

Jim snorted derisively. 'Ridiculous!'

'Ridiculous!' echoed the DJ. *'How are they going to manage that? Sounds like a logistical nightmare, doesn't it?'*

'A plonking understatement,' muttered Jim.

'This is a tournament like no other, my friends. Every match is a contest of sudden death. First team to score goes through. Each match will be decided by a single golden goal.'

'Raaah!' Flint smacked the dashboard. 'Amazing! What a brilliant scary idea.'

'I like it!' screeched the DJ. *'Sudden death, all the way through to the final where the winners get to play the league*

champions in a full-length match. There's prize money, the chance for a place in the league, and silverware. A great big cup, aptly named the Blanchard Trophy, is sitting right in front of me. And let me tell you, it is a thing of beauty. For details of how to enter this fabulous tournament, phone our hotline. Or call into Blanchards and pick up an entry form.'

'Arrogant vainglorious opportunistic self-publicizing showman!' Jim stabbed the on-off button.

They drove in silence.

'I'm sorry,' said Jim. 'I've been irritable lately.'

Flint glanced. 'I hadn't noticed.'

Jim shook his head. 'There've been difficulties and disagreements at the club. I didn't want to involve you in it. It's complicated . . . stupid.' His hands tapped anxiously on the steering wheel. 'I've been a lousy dad.'

'I don't think so,' said Flint. 'If anyone should be apologizing, it's me.'

Jim gave a loud snort. 'Now you're being ridiculous!'

Flint couldn't quite bring himself to list his offences – the run-in with the police, the on-pitch fight with Aldo and sending off, sneaking out at night, the drainpipe and the fall from the second-storey window. 'I'm sorry anyway,' he mumbled.

Turning in through the club's grand gateway, Jim cruised the car up to the clubhouse and parked. He reached his arm around Flint's shoulders. 'You're a good lad.'

'Hey.' Flint grinned. 'And you're not a bad dad.'

Jim hugged him.

'Excellent timing!' From the clubhouse steps, Roger Blanchard strode purposefully towards the car. He leered through the open window. 'Just been trying to get you on the phone. Wife said you were on your way down.'

'Flint and I were just going to work through a few new drills,' said Jim.

'Sorry.' Blanchard shook his head sternly. 'Emergency committee meeting. Just about to convene.'

Jim scowled. 'Talk about short notice. Who called it?'

'Whole bunch of us really.' Blanchard looked away.

'Sorry, mate.' Jim slapped Flint's leg. 'Looks like you're on your own. I'll try and be as quick as I can.' Turning to Blanchard, he sighed wearily. 'What's this one about then?'

'Dismissal.'

'Dismissal?' Jim stiffened. 'Whose?'

Blanchard's face was cold granite. 'Yours.'

CHAPTER 13
THE LAST STRAW

'Victimizing and favouritism!'

'That's the way it goes.' Jim banged down his mug on the crowded workbench as if to reinforce his point: the matter was closed.

'I can't believe you're just going to roll over and let them do this to you!' Flint kicked a rusty-looking piece of machinery. 'What about that famous fighting spirit you're always going on about in training sessions?'

Jim sighed, exasperated. 'Do you want a lift or not?' The Eyesore, his shed, was also his retreat — the place he went when thinking needed to be done. Having thought things through, he would not be drawn.

'How can they accuse you of victimizing Aldo?' Flint smacked his palm against the side of the workbench. 'That's ridiculous! You've shown the patience of a saint! He's twice as arrogant as he is talented. If you'd've given me more chances to play I would have shown him.'

Jim grunted. 'Now I've gone, hopefully, you'll get those opportunities. It was hard for me to treat you fairly.'

'Exactly – accusing you of favouritism, that's absurd. When did you ever show me any?'

Jim shrugged. 'The committee's decision was unanimous.'

'You've fallen over backwards', said Flint, 'trying to ensure you never gave me special treatment. If anything, you went too far the other way.'

Jim's smile was fleeting. 'The people that count don't seem to see it that way.'

'It's the truth!'

'Truth, I'm afraid, doesn't come into it.'

'In practically every practice session I outperformed Aldo. But I had to wait all this time before getting a chance in the team.'

'That wasn't entirely down to me.' Jim rubbed weariness from his eyes. 'Blanchard has stitched me up. Ever since he arrived he's wanted to get rid of me. And now, in cahoots with Llewellyn and the rest of that miserable pack, he's done it.'

'Because you disagree with what he's doing at the club?'

Jim nodded. 'I was in the way. Now I understand why he was so enthusiastic when I asked about you joining the club.' He groaned. 'I'm so stupid. He's used you to get me out. Even roped his son in on it. Been planning it all the way along.'

'But you're innocent!' Flint scowled. Frustrated. 'Can't you take them to court or something?'

'It'd take years and cost a fortune,' said Jim. 'They'd win.' He shook his head. 'It's done. There's nothing I can do about it.'

'If you're not there,' said Flint, 'I don't want to be either. I'm not going to play for a club that treats people like that.'

'Now steady on.' Jim leaned forward. 'If you miss out on the opportunity to train and play, how's that going to help matters?' He put a hand on Flint's shoulder. 'I've not felt at home there for a long time, sooner or later I was going to have to leave. But you're in there. You're a member. They've got the best facilities of any club in the region. It'd be daft to give all that up.'

'But the coaching . . .'

'It's time I took a break.' Jim smiled. 'Anyway, it's not as if I'm going to be idle – we can still work on stuff when you're not at the club. And I'll be coming along to watch. That'll keep me busy. I'll be like all the other dads – rooting for my son. It's going to be great!'

Flint gulped down water and wiped his face on his shirt one more time. He was dripping sweat. Llewellyn, trying to stamp his authority on the first team, had pushed them hard in the warm-up session. So hard that, now they were actually playing, everyone was knackered. What was the point in that?

'OK, lads,' Llewellyn blew his whistle. 'On we go. Change ends.'

Slooshing his mouth out with water, Flint spat it at the ground. Llewellyn must realize how tired they were. He was doing this to let them know who was boss.

Jim had always been constructive, encouraging his players. If he criticized a boy for a move that had failed to come off, he would always try to suggest a more appropriate approach, or a better technique. But that wasn't Llewellyn's style.

'Come on now, Flint! *Wakey-wakey!*' Llewellyn pointed down the pitch. 'Let's have your mind back on the game. You've had your rest.'

The first team had dispossessed the reserves and were already advancing at a steady pace into their half. Sprinting up the middle of the pitch, Flint watched Matt curve a long ball in towards Aldo.

Aldo manoeuvred for it, but before he had the ball under control, Moses, the smallest and fastest of the reserve defenders, nipped it cleanly away and hoofed it. As the whistle blew for a throw in, Aldo spun round, exasperated. 'Where were you?' he glared at Flint. 'Who am I supposed to pass to when they box me in!?'

Flint glanced around at his fellow midfielders, both of them in as good a position as himself. Aldo could have passed to any one of them if he hadn't been tackled first. 'I'm here, aren't I?' Flint made as if to measure the distance between him and Aldo. 'How close d'you need me? Perhaps you'd like me to wave a big flag next time?'

Aldo's eyes narrowed, his fists clenched.

'Buck your ideas up, Flint.' Llewellyn came running over. 'Come on, the pair of you. We haven't got time for squabbling.'

Flint shot Llewellyn a furious glance.

It was the first team's throw. Looking for a good position, Flint glanced over to where Jim was standing with a couple of the other dads, watching from the touchline.

Llewellyn cupped his hands to his mouth. 'Let's move it up a gear. I want to see you boys hungry for that ball!'

Matt took the throw, launching the ball deep into the reserves' half. Galvanizing himself, Flint took off at a pace. Llewellyn wanted hungry, did he? Ahead, Aldo sprinted into the box, turning to see where the ball had got to. A pass was already in the air – high and long. Flint charged, dodging his way between the defenders.

'Go on, Aldo!' Llewellyn's yell. 'Smash it home!'

In front of the goal, Aldo leaped and headed. Escaping the keeper's outstretched arms, his ball ricocheted off the crossbar. *'Mine!'* Aldo's leg slashed reflexively at the air. Flint dived . . .

'*Yeees!*'

'*Lovely!*'

Flint had barely slid to a halt, when a hand tugged roughly at his collar. He rolled over on his back.

'*Idiot!* Didn't you hear me call?' Aldo spat with rage. 'That was *my* ball!'

'Says?' Flint leapt to his feet. 'You had your chance! You missed!'

Players from both sides turned to watch.

Aldo's scowl was ugly. 'You were in my way!' He pushed Flint backwards.

Fists clenched, Flint returned the shove. 'You should have banged it home the first time.'

'OK! That's enough!' Llewellyn's flushed face loomed into view. Forcing himself between the two boys, he turned to Flint. 'That's enough!'

'His dad doesn't own the club,' snapped Flint.

'I said that's enough.'

'Aldo doesn't own the ball.'

'Enough!'

'He thinks he's so special,' hissed Flint. 'But he's a jumped up little no-talent.'

'*Right!*' Grabbing Flint's shoulders, Llewellyn shook. 'That's *it*! You've had your warnings. I've put up with all I'm going to take from you! Get showered! Get changed! Wait for me outside the clubhouse.'

As the big hands released him, Flint stared, shocked. Llewellyn's eyes seemed to bulge in their sockets.

'*Move*, boy!' Llewellyn clapped his hands. 'Jump!'

'Hang on!' Jim approached at a run. 'Just a minute.'

Llewellyn span round.

'You can't do that.' Patting Flint's shoulder, Jim scowled at Llewellyn.

'Can't!?' Llewellyn's face darkened further. 'I'm in charge here now,' he spluttered. 'You've no right to interfere.'

'Don't I?' Jim's voice was calm, masking an undercurrent of fury. He stepped up close to Llewellyn, a direct challenge. 'What d'you think you're doing? You were shaking a child.'

Players had gathered. Flint felt angry and embarrassed. He glanced at Jim. 'It's OK.' He shrugged. 'I'm all right.'

Llewellyn looked uncomfortable. He glared at Jim. 'I was trying to restore some order.' His jaw clenched. 'Which *you* are now disrupting. Would you please leave the pitch.' He turned to Flint. 'And you do as I asked.'

Flint recognized one of the fathers who had been standing beside Jim. Accompanied by Blanchard, he was hurrying back towards the pitch.

'What's going on?' roared Blanchard.

Llewellyn nodded towards Jim. 'Mr Baker is disrupting my training session.'

Blanchard fixed furious eyes on Jim. 'OK, that's enough.' He pointed towards the gate. 'Off you go! This is club property. You have no right to be here. You don't coach for Welbeck any more.'

Jim folded his arms. 'True enough – I'm no longer the coach.' His eyes flitted towards the fathers on the touchline. 'But I have the same rights they do.'

'Do you indeed.' Blanchard glared. 'And what rights are those, then?'

'I came to watch my son.'

'Your son!' Blanchard snorted. 'Your *son?*'

'Flint's been sent off.' Llewellyn's tone was curt. 'He was on his way to the club-house.'

'Hear that?' Blanchard took a step

towards Jim. 'Flint's services are no longer required today. I suggest you take your *son* home.'

Turning his back on his teammates, Flint started walking.

CHAPTER 14
TOAST

'Flint!' Sandra dropped the knife and the piece of toast. 'Hello stranger!' Beaming the big smile, she wrapped her arms around him and hugged. 'How lovely to see you!' She squeezed him half to death, released him and stepped back. 'Let me take a look.' The eyes measured. 'Has Janet not been feeding you? I swear you've lost weight!'

Flint shook his head. 'You just squished me.' He laughed. 'I'm eating plenty.'

'I'm sure you are.' Sandra grinned. 'Only kidding.' The smile gave way to a look of hurt. 'Don't suppose you're here to see your old keyworker though.'

'Course I am!'

'A likely story.' Sandra smiled again – she was teasing. Picking up the knife, she returned to buttering the pile of toast. 'If you're looking for Beanie, I'm afraid she's out.'

'I wasn't particularly.' Flint took a knife from the drawer and joined in.

Sandra stopped and stared. 'Is something wrong?'

'No.'

Sandra frowned. 'Let me put that another way. Is everything all right?'

'Why shouldn't it be?'

'Why? Because you turn up here saying you've not come to see Beanie. And then, without me having to ask, you take a knife from the drawer and start helping me butter toast. That's why. It's not like you. Something has to be going on.'

Flint shrugged. 'Actually you could pass on a message to Beanie for me.'

'What's that?'

'There's a football competition. Tell her she and her mates can enter. It's open to anyone that can get a team together. There's prize money, a big trophy and everything. But she'll have to go to Blanchards to get the entry form.'

'Blanchards? Isn't that the place . . . ?'

Flint smirked. 'Yeah. They're the ones sponsoring it. There was a telephone number but I didn't manage to write it down.'

'OK.' Grabbing a pen and a scrap of paper from her back pocket, Sandra scribbled a note. 'You, Janet and Jim still getting along OK?'

'Of course.' Flint nodded. 'They're great.'

'Janet might be a little stiff, but she's a lovely woman,' said Sandra. 'One parent is often easier to get to know than the other. Easier to get close to. Give it time.'

'She's fine,' said Flint.

Sandra smiled. 'I really liked Jim. So full of energy and enthusiasm. Such a generous heart. They're a lovely couple. You're very lucky.'

'I know.' Flint could feel Sandra's eyes watching him, reading him. 'D'you want some more toast making?'

'There's something on your mind.'

Flint looked away.

'You can tell me about it. Is it to do with Jim?'

'How did you know?' Flint sighed.

Sandra touched his shoulder. 'It's my job, silly.'

'That business with the club . . .' He had

called Sandra the day Jim was dropped by the club. But now he was wary of saying anything that might give her concerns, make her think about bringing him back to Bella. 'The way they've treated him is terrible.'

'Jim's not taking it too well, huh?' Sandra shook her head. 'I'm not surprised, poor guy. The club was his passion.'

'He used to moan sometimes,' said Flint, 'about how the club had changed and wasn't the way it should be. It used to get to him. He talked about it maybe being time for him to move on or take a break because it took up all his free time. But now he's out of there . . .'

'It's affecting him?'

Flint nodded. 'He's just not the same. You can see it in his eyes. Some days its like there's nobody there.'

'It's bound to take him time to adjust,' said Sandra. 'He still coaches you and goes to watch you play?'

'Yeah, but . . . I'm training with the club most evenings.' Flint sighed again. 'He hides away in his shed. I heard him shouting on the phone – I think he lost his job last week because he didn't bother to show up. At meal-times he hardly touches his food.'

'Not eating!' Sandra made a tutting sound. 'Now that's *serious*!' Sandra believed above all else that people should eat properly. 'I can see I'll have to have a word with Mr Baker. We can't have your new dad wasting away.'

Flint chewed his lip. Had he done the right thing telling Sandra? Maybe he shouldn't have come.

'Here!' Sandra handed him a slice of buttered toast. 'Eat this. Much tastier than your own flesh. Don't you worry. We'll sort this out. I'm due to make a visit anyways.'

That was what worried him. What would she make of Jim? What would she decide? He couldn't bear to move back into 'care'.

CHAPTER 15
BIG MATCH

First corner of the big match – a win would put Welbeck beyond reach, unassailable, champions of the league. Drayton's penalty area crackled with tension. There had been plenty of to-ing and fro-ing, but so far neither side had scored. The two teams appeared evenly matched: both were searching for that early advantage.

A corner might lead to a goal. So might any shot, but being awarded a corner was like having your army allowed to march right into the heart of enemy territory and prepare themselves in the best strategic positions ready to do battle – all with minimal harassment from the enemy.

Flint had resigned himself to being so tightly shadowed he could smell his marker's hair gel. As far as he was concerned, the hilarious frantic jostling for position that went on was a waste of time and energy. At the last second, just before the kicker struck the ball, he would evade his marker as he always did. The important thing was to be aware of everyone around you, spot the cracks when they opened, and of course *anticipate where the ball was heading*.

'Hey, Flint...'

He jerked round.

'It was me that got rid of your dad.' Aldo stared, pure malevolence.

Flint laughed dismissively. But the uncomfortable thought was planted.

Aldo knocked into him. 'And guess who's next!'

'Oh yeah!' Flint refused to be psyched. 'I forgot you run this club.' He glanced over to where home supporters had gathered behind the goal-line. A familiar face beamed reassuringly from the crowd.

'Come on, Welbeck!' roared Jim. 'Give us a goal!' Home supporters echoed his call. He made a clenched fist. 'All the way, my son!'

Flint felt a flutter of pride. It meant the world to Jim that he was out here playing in the team. He could weather Aldo's pathetic rivalry, his provocations and little tantrums. Let Aldo play his silly games; only one game mattered: *football*.

The whistle blew. Matt took a deep breath and started his run at the ball. In the box, the jostling grew frenzied. Twisting away from his marker, Flint cut across the throng towards the unguarded back post.

The ball came low, but with power and spin, cutting an arc across the front of the box. Legs thrashed wildly, defenders flung themselves, but somehow it kept on till Aldo dropped backwards, redirecting it with his deadly right. In a blink, Flint followed suit, a somersault kick to put the ball on target.

The world span.

'*Yeeeeeees!*'

It was in the net.

Jubilant teammates hurled themselves on Flint. 'Unbelievable!' 'The best!' 'Where did you pull that from?' When he finally rolled free and struggled to his feet, the home supporters were still celebrating.

Behind the goal Jim grinned and

punched the air. 'Way to go! That's got to be a first. Twin overhead volleys. Never seen a goal like it. Astonishing!'

Dazed, looking around, Flint spotted Aldo. Teammates were congratulating him too, but he wasn't celebrating; he'd been upstaged. Flint couldn't resist a smile.

Aldo scowled. He looked ready to say something. But suddenly everyone was turning.

'Take your hands off me!'

Flint span round.

'How dare you!' Jim was yelling at Blanchard and struggling to break free from two men who were attempting to restrain him. The men – one tall, one fat – were wearing fluorescent stewards bibs.

Flint dashed.

'I've already made it clear . . .' Blanchard's finger jabbed the air in front of Jim. 'You're no longer welcome at Welbeck. Your presence on this touchline undermines the coach.'

'Poppycock!' snarled Jim.

Blanchard was trying to stay calm. 'The club doesn't want you here.'

'Club? Pah! *You*, you mean. You and your fat-cat cronies.' The muscles and veins stood out on Jim's neck. 'You have absolutely no right!' he snarled, twisting and scowling at his restrainers.

'Let go of him!' Flint lunged at the fat man. But the fat man shoved him away.

'Whoa!' Blanchard caught hold of Flint. 'Now hang on. Jim has been asked politely.'

'Take your hands off him!' roared Jim. 'I'm not going anywhere. I'm here to watch my son play football. I've as much right as any of these parents.'

Flint glanced around. Faces. Home and away supporters, both the teams and their coaches, the referee and linesmen – everyone was staring. The referee stepped forward, stern-faced. 'This is totally unacceptable!' he barked. 'This stops immediately or I cancel the game.'

Flint felt Blanchard's grip release.

'Absolutely.' Blanchard blushed and nodded. 'My apologies. It's a bit of an awkward situation – all very embarrassing. If you could just give us a minute . . . ?'

The referee scowled and glanced over towards Drayton's coach.

The coach shrugged resignedly and nodded.

'OK.' The referee tapped his watch. 'One

minute. No more.' He waved the gathered players back onto the pitch. 'Come on. Let's have you in your positions ready to start.'

Blanchard gestured to the two men holding Jim.

The men released Jim's arms. Flint ran to his side. Together they followed Blanchard away from the touchline.

Blanchard turned to face Jim. 'Listen carefully. I've checked – the club's constitution allows for a boy's real parents to attend matches and give their support. But makes no such provision for the likes of carers or foster parents. Sorry, old man.'

Jim looked shaken. 'I don't believe you.'

'I've a copy in the clubhouse,' said Blanchard tersely. 'I'll show you, but you have to give me your word there'll be no more embarrassing nonsense.'

'OK.' Jim patted Flint's shoulder. 'Go on, mate, the ref's waiting. I'll be back soon. Score us some goals.'

Psychologically, Welbeck's opening goal – the double overhead volley special – should have finished Drayton off. But the off-pitch argument between Jim and Blanchard had distracted everybody and the incredible power of that magical moment had been lost. It took a while, but when Drayton scored their equalizer, Welbeck's aura of skilful invulnerability was dashed.

Once they saw their opponents were not gods, Drayton set about punishing them. With their confidence up, they played like a different team. Welbeck couldn't get a touch. They were being played off the pitch. And both they and their new coach knew it. 'Come on!' yelled Llewellyn from the touchline. 'Pull yourselves together. *Get stuck in!'*

The first half had turned into a rout – Drayton had bagged a second, and then a third – and there was still time to go. Welbeck were tired of chasing the ball with no result, tired of running into bad luck losing the ball, miskicking shots, hitting the crossbar and post, over and over . . . They had lost faith in themselves and, though they had begun the game as favourites and got off to a brilliant start, not one of them now believed they could turn things around.

And as if that wasn't enough, an ambulance had come racing up the drive to the clubhouse, lights flashing but no siren. Every boy on the pitch kept turning for a glimpse of who had been injured in one of the other matches.

'Keep your minds on the game!' Llewellyn's voice was charged with exasperation. 'Let's see some tackling. They're not going to *give* you the ball, Welbeck. Come *on!* Where's the enthusiasm?'

Flint felt Llewellyn's dagger-eyes, they'd been on him a lot. He'd forced himself to run, to harass, to tackle, to chase the ball, but his heart had not been in it. It had felt like he'd just been going through the motions: there was no will, no drive, he'd not been focused on the game. The argument between Jim and Blanchard had left him with a bad feeling. His eyes kept flitting towards the touchline, straying at every opportunity towards the clubhouse. *Shake it off.*

'Flint!' It was Aldo, furious, pointing to the wing. 'Wake up, you dope!'

Flint turned. Close by, besieged by Drayton players, little Moses, newly promoted to the first team, was twisting and turning in a desperate struggle to retain possession. 'Moses!' Sprinting, Flint signalled. 'Pass it!' He moved in closer. 'Come on!' Moses was being hacked down, but there was no whistle from the ref. In one last heroic effort, Moses poked the ball clear as he fell.

Flint felt energy kick in. Rage. Racing the Drayton players to the ball, he tore between them. They tried to pull him down, they grabbed at his shirt, blocked his path, hacked at his feet. Flint dropped his shoulder low and crashed them aside, relishing the impact. It was as if he'd been sleepwalking for the last twenty minutes and now he was suddenly wide awake.

He glanced around. Teammates were scattered in defensive positions. Even Aldo was further back. The team looked tired and hangdog. 'Come *on*!' yelled Flint, keeping one eye on the Drayton players closing from all sides. Dummying, he back-heeled to Matt. 'You and me!' he yelled and took off at a sprint into Drayton territory.

Matt charged down the wing. It was what he did best. Flint pushed his way through the Drayton midfield and glanced across. The ball was in the air, Matt was on the ground, fouled. Whistle in mouth, the ref waited to see if the ball might fall to Welbeck's advantage.

Flint scrambled to get beneath it. Barged and crushed from all sides, he couldn't make it – the ball hit the ground and bounced high. He shoved and ducked his way free, got the goal in his sights and, as it came back down a second time, shot.

'*At last!*'

From twenty metres.

'*Yeeeees!*'

'*Fantastic!*'

Welbeck's supporters had waited a long time for the second goal. Now it had finally arrived, they gave loud voice to their delight.

'*Excellent!*' Llewellyn struggled to make himself heard through the cheers. 'That's more like it. Come on, the rest of you. Does Flint have to do all the work? I want that equalizer before . . .'

The referee's whistle cut Llewellyn short. *Half-time*.

Weary, the players headed back to the clubhouse; it was time to top up with fluids, have a brief sit down and get an earful from the coach. Uplifted by his turn-around, Flint walked in with Matt and Moses, the three of them had worked well together.

'I don't get it.' Aldo jogged up alongside Matt, wearing the predictable scowl.

'You don't, do you?' said Flint.

Aldo pointed an accusing finger. 'Flint staggers about like some clumsy fool, and we do our best to plug the holes he's leaving all over the midfield. Then, when the rest of us are worn out, he snatches glory with a lucky shot.' He spat at the ground. 'And who does Llewellyn praise?'

Flint stopped dead in his tracks.

Aldo squared up to him. 'Nothing to say for yourself?'

Matt and Moses exchanged glances.

Rooted to the spot, Flint stared straight ahead.

Blue lights flashed. Carrying a stretcher out through the clubhouse doors, two paramedics pushed their way through a bustle of people to the waiting ambulance. The face of the figure on the stretcher was covered by an oxygen mask, the skin was a horrible blue grey . . . but there was no mistaking the identity.

Flint ran. *'Jim!'*

CHAPTER 16
INTENSIVE CARE

A cute myocardial infarkshun.

Flint pressed his face against the glass. Jim's arms and chest had sprouted tubes and wires; his mouth and nose were covered by an oxygen mask. His eyes were closed, his body still and grey as stone. The only signs of life came from the rack of bedside monitors – little flickering lights and an illuminated green tadpole tracing a pulse-line across a dark screen.

A cute myocardial infarkshun. Something like that. The man in the white coat, the specialist doctor who had been in charge of the nurses and other medical people looking after Jim, had used the phrase. Flint had tried to picture what it might mean and how it connected with Jim. Finally he had interrupted the doctor and asked what this 'cute' thing was.

The doctor had stalled, looked perplexed, apologized and written the phrase on a piece of paper for him. *Acute myocardial infarction* he explained was the medical term for a *heart attack*.

'The doctors and nurses all look so terribly young.' Janet's voice quivered. She had looked like a ghost when she arrived at the hospital – pale face, eyes dark hollows. She had seemed bewildered, but determined to be strong: asking pertinent questions and trying to take everything in. Everything had been so hectic, so urgent, a life and death *emergency*. She and he had kept themselves clenched and separate.

Flint turned. Janet was standing next to him, her eyes glued to the figure in the bed on the other side of the glass. A tear wormed its way down her cheek. In the glaring green-tinged light she looked unbearably frail. If he touched her she might break. He reached out his hand to the small of her back.

Janet didn't move.

Another tear welled and rolled. Flint felt

a faint tremor beneath his hand. From her core it seemed to come, spreading outwards till her whole body shook. And still Janet stared through the glass, the tears coming faster, trembling as they fell.

Flint felt his own eyes pricking, felt a tremble building in his own chest. He knew if he looked again through the glass, if he saw Jim lying there stricken, lifeless as a corpse, the awful churning feeling would burst out, and an uncontrollable torrent would begin. So he stroked Janet's back.

Suddenly, with a big shuddering sigh, Janet turned and wrapped her arms around him. And like two lost souls, they clung to each other and wept.

CHAPTER 17
ANGER

Folding his arms beneath the seat belt, Flint turned to the window and watched the passing street whizz by.

'They were both right,' said Sandra. 'Janet and the doctor. You can't hang around at the hospital twenty-four hours a day, seven days a week.'

Flint grunted. After a night and a day, he and Janet had taken a taxi home to sleep. Jim's eyes had still been closed when they'd returned in the morning.

'We don't know how long it's going to take for Jim to get better.' Sandra glanced across as she slowed the car for traffic lights. 'You know him much better than I do. Think he'd want you to spend all your time sitting around in the hospital, waiting for him to stir?'

Flint shrugged.

'I don't think so,' said Sandra. 'In fact I'm pretty sure he'd be the first to insist you carry on with your life. He wouldn't want you missing football training, would he?' She was trying to sound buoyant. 'You must be dying to find out how your team got on.'

Flint glowered.

'Oh God! *Dying.*' Sandra smacked the steering wheel. 'I'm sorry. Unfortunate phrase. Stupid language. I'm *really* sorry.' Shaking her head, she bit her lip and scowled at the traffic.

No-one from Welbeck club had visited the hospital. But there had been a message on the answerphone at home: Mrs Lees, club secretary, expressing the club's 'heartfelt concern'. Offering everyone's condolences, she wanted Jim's family to know that all at Welbeck would be hoping and praying for the speediest possible recovery.

Flint doubted it. He knew there were people at the club who wanted Jim out of the way. And as for how the first team had faired after his sudden half-time departure in the back of the ambulance with Jim – this was the first moment he'd thought about it. He didn't care about the club or the team, he had never really felt part of either. Whether they had won or lost against Drayton now held no interest for him whatsoever.

'Here we are!' Turning off the main road, Sandra steered through the gates and cruised up the drive to the clubhouse. 'I could stay and watch if you like.' Pulling on the hand-brake, she slipped the car out of gear and leant back in the corner of her seat so she could look at him.

'Suit yourself.' Flint avoided eye contact. 'It's just a practice session. I don't care.'

'Hey!' Sandra touched his arm. 'Don't be like that. I thought you might like someone around.' Her voice was gentle, placating. 'Are you angry with me?'

Flint shook his head.

'But you are angry?'

Flint shrugged.

'With the world maybe?'

'Maybe.' Flint frowned.

'You've every right to be.' Sandra leant across. 'D'you want a hug?'

'No thanks.' He so desperately wanted one. But a hug would bring it all to the surface again: he'd dissolve, become a blubbering wreck. He needed to be strong.

'Sure?'

He nodded.

'OK.' Sandra pressed the release on Flint's seat belt. 'Go and do your training. I'll drive round to the car park and wait there.' She smiled. 'Don't worry – I won't get bored.' She nodded to a pile of folders on the back seat. 'Plenty of reports to keep me busy!' With a quick lick of her thumbs she slicked down his eyebrows.

Flint tried to find a smile. 'Thanks.' He opened the door. 'See you later.'

It felt wrong being at the club. Not because he should have been at the hospital waiting by Jim's bedside, but because he didn't belong. He had thought he could fit in, but Stretch had been right – he was an outsider at Welbeck and always would be. From time to time, one or two of his teammates had been friendly enough, but Aldo resented him, and his influence over the squad was too strong. As long as he was there, that wouldn't alter.

The changing room was crowded and noisy, the squad were mostly already in their kit and making final adjustments to boots and shin pads. Flint was late. Heads turned and conversations stalled as he pushed his way through, looking for somewhere to hang his clothes.

In conversation with Aldo, Llewellyn nodded stiffly. 'Flint. Good to have you back.'

Flint plonked down his bag and wearily tugged at his shirt.

Llewellyn was instructing Aldo to take the squad out and lead the warm-up routine whilst he dealt with some urgent matter in the clubhouse. As he headed for the door, he paused by Flint. 'I want you and Aldo working together. Put your differences behind you.' He left in a hurry before Flint could reply.

'Hey, Flinty.'

Flint turned.

Aldo stepped forward, glancing round for an audience. 'Old Jim Baker was a touch premature wasn't he?' He was smirking, looking for laughs.

'Premature?' Flint took a deep breath. 'What do you mean?'

Aldo leered. 'I thought the Sudden Death was supposed to be in July.'

There was a horrible crunching sound. Followed by a long and very loud groan. Everybody in the room froze. Aldo staggered, clutching his face. 'Bastard!' He spat with blood.

Droplets speckled Flint's skin. He stepped back, wiping his forehead.

Aldo squealed loudly, trying to make the pain go away. In shocked silence the others looked on. Trickling thickly through Aldo's fingers, blood dripped and splattered the floor.

The door rattled. Llewellyn rushed in breathless. 'What on earth . . . ?'

Flint snatched up his bag. 'Someone else can tell you.' He barged past. 'I'm through with this club.'

Flint knocked.

Noises inside, Beanie scurrying to the door. 'Who is it?'

'Flint.'

The door swung open. 'Long time no see!' Beanie smiled. 'What you doing here?'

'Can I come in?'

'Of course.' Beanie beckoned, went over to the window and sat on the floor like she always did.

The room smelt faintly of cigarette smoke. Flint sat on her bed. 'I'm sorry I've not been round much, but . . .'

'It's all right.' She grinned. 'You know

me – I'm never here except when I have to be: to eat and to sleep and stuff. I didn't really expect to see you down the old house. You and Stretch aren't exactly the best of mates. He's not the easiest of people.' She peered. 'Jeeeez! You look terrible, Flint. Is that . . . ? Oh, my God – blood! What's been going on?'

'Everything.' Flint shook his head wearily. He took a long deep breath. 'The blood's not mine. I hit someone.'

'What!'

'This boy at the football club.' Flint groaned. 'The team captain. I nutted him.'

'You?' Beanie's eyes and mouth widened with shock. 'I don't believe it!'

'I know.' Flint nodded. 'My days with Welbeck are well and truly over.'

'No!' Beanie shook her head. 'That pukka team? What happened?'

'He made a joke about Jim.' Flint's voice croaked. 'About him dying.'

'That's out of order.'

'Jim's in intensive care.'

'*What!?*' Beanie jumped to her feet.

Flint nodded. 'Heart attack.' He swallowed. 'I think he's dying, Bean.'

Diving on the bed, Beanie hugged him. 'He can't be! You only just got him.'

Flint hid his face behind his hands. 'I'm scared . . .'

Beanie pressed her face against Flint's fingers, nuzzling. 'He's not going to die.'

'You don't know that.'

'He can't! They check out people before they let them foster.' Beanie tried to pry away the fingers. 'They have to be healthy. Jim'll recover. It'll just be some kind of freak thing. Believe me.'

Flint wanted to. He badly wanted to. But he'd been here before . . . 'Freak things kill people.'

Janet poured tea. She looked small and tired, but the familiar straight back and tight, tense expression were back in place.

Flint pulled out a chair and sat at the table. 'I have to tell you something.'

Janet raised an eyebrow. 'Sandra informed me about your little incident when she called.' Her voice was weary. She carried Flint's mug over to the table. 'No cards from the football club for Jim.' She managed a little smile. 'But I expect we'll be getting a letter about you.'

Flint bowed his head. 'I'm sorry.'

Janet sat down with her mug. 'Well I

can't say I approve of the method you used to express yourself, but by all accounts you were provoked. I expect you'll have to do some serious apologizing to get back in the team.'

'I don't want to.'

'Sometimes we have to say sorry even when we don't want to, or when we think it's unfair.'

Flint shook his head. 'I meant I don't want to go back there. I'm done with Welbeck. No-one even asked about Jim.'

Janet gave a small nod. 'Talking of whom . . .'

'There's another thing.'

Janet frowned.

'This is difficult . . .' Flint cleared his throat. 'I hope you won't take it the wrong way but . . . I don't want to go back to the hospital.'

'But . . .'

'I've been through this before.'

Janet blushed. 'Of course.' She reached across and clasped his hand. 'Your mother.'

Flint looked down at his lap. 'She was hooked up to all those tubes and things, just like Jim.' His bottom lip trembled. 'We waited . . .'

'Her eyes never opened?'

Flint shook his head.

'I'm so sorry . . .' Janet sighed and squeezed his hand. 'That must have been so awful for you . . . unbearable.' She leant close across the table. 'But that's what I've been trying to tell you . . .'

Flint looked up.

'Jim's eyes are open!'

Flint felt his heart flutter. 'Open?'

Janet nodded. 'When I left he was sitting up in bed.' She beamed. 'Wide awake!'

CHAPTER 18
DOCTOR

'No wheelchairs for me!' Jim made his way, shuffling slowly but surely, to the end of the bed, then sat with a grunt. He looked around. Janet, Flint and Charlie, the talkative old man in the bed opposite, clapped and cheered; some of the other patients managed a nod or a weak smile in show of support.

'Excellent!' Dr Richards came briskly walking, cheerfully smiling, down the ward. 'Up and running!'

'I don't know about you lot . . .' Jim's voice had almost returned to full strength over the days he had spent recovering, but there was still a little hint of tiredness. He smiled to his audience. 'I wouldn't exactly call that *running*.'

Richards, Janet and Flint laughed.

Charlie chuckled. 'It may not be Olympic standard but...' He wheezed and coughed. 'Right now, young Jimmy, you're the fastest on the ward.'

'A point well made,' said Richards. He patted Jim's shoulder. 'One day at a time, my friend.'

With another grunt, Jim pushed back up onto his feet and shuffled to the end of Charlie's bed. 'As soon as you're up and about, old-timer,' he said, 'you and me are going to have a race!'

Janet picked up the small pile of Jim's clothes she had neatly folded. 'Listen to them, doctor! I think some of those tablets you've been giving them have affected their poor minds! Come on . . .' She took hold of Jim's arm. 'We've got a long walk ahead of us. Say goodbye to your mates.'

Jim put his hand on Janet's. 'Thank you.' He shook his head. 'But I want to try and do this on my own.'

Janet's eyes flitted anxiously towards Dr Richards. The doctor shrugged.

Jim straightened his back. 'Just to the

lift.' He smiled. 'I'll take it slowly.'

'OK.' It was almost a whisper. Janet stepped back. 'Gently.'

Jim winked. 'Don't worry. I'll be fine. I'll wait for you.'

Janet nodded.

Taking a couple of tentative steps Jim turned and raised his hand in a wave. 'I'll be back, you guys.' A few steps more, he turned and grinned. 'Just to visit, mind.'

Charlie and the boys smiled and nodded.

Watching Jim make his way down the ward, Flint willed him not to falter or fall. Such courage and determination.

Dr Richards came to stand beside him. 'He shows tremendous spirit. An excellent sign.' The doctor leant against the white tubular bedstead. 'Jim's been telling me: he's immensely proud of his son.'

'His son?'

Dr Richards looked embarrassed. 'You,' he said. 'I've heard all about your exploits on the pitch . . . at the club.'

'I haven't told him.' Flint chewed at a broken nail. 'I thought it best not to.'

'Told him what?' said Richards.

'I don't play for Welbeck any more.'

'No?' The doctor looked puzzled. 'That's a shame. Why not?'

'I couldn't,' said Flint. 'Not after the way they treated him. They got rid of him – he objected to their plans to make the club more upmarket and they didn't like it. Losing the coaching job really affected him. And then they wouldn't let him stay to watch me play. That's what's done this to him.'

'I see . . .' Richards frowned.

'He built the team,' said Flint. 'It meant a lot to him once. But the club had changed. It wasn't good for him.'

'No,' said Richards. 'It doesn't sound like it.' His brow furrowed. 'Maybe we can think of something else for him to focus his energy and enthusiasm on.'

'How d'you mean?'

'I've had cases like this before,' said the doctor. 'What you've told me doesn't surprise me. Jim's a proud man. He puts his heart into things.'

Flint nodded.

'He's suffered a couple of big blows,' said Richards. 'If he's going to make a good recovery, apart from exercise and diet regimes, he needs something that will give him a boost, something he can care about, something he can put his heart into again.'

Jim had made it as far as the end of the

ward, he turned, waved stiffly and turned the corner into the corridor.

'Thank you, Dr Richards.' Janet smiled. 'Thank you for everything.' She turned to Flint. 'Come on. We'd better go. Don't want him running off.'

Richards winked at Flint. 'Give it some thought, heh? Maybe you can come up with something.'

CHAPTER 19
IDEA

Over the last two weeks, watching Jim's very slow progress, Flint had given Dr Richards's words a lot of thought.

As he walked in, eyes flickered, conversations died and the room fell silent. Stretch and Beanie were on the sofa with their backs to him, talking to Nidge and a couple of the other boys. Nidge nudged Stretch. Stretch glanced round and nudged Beanie. Beanie jumped up. 'Flint!'

Flint gave a curt nod. He had reached the middle of the room. He turned to survey the mostly familiar faces, his gaze resting finally on Stretch.

'Long time, no see,' said Stretch.

Flint nodded. 'You and me didn't exactly see eye-to-eye . . .'

Stretch smiled. 'We had our little differences.'

Flint cleared his throat. 'You despise me.'

Beanie glared at Stretch.

Stretch shifted uncomfortably. 'I wouldn't say that exactly . . .'

'Look,' snapped Flint, 'it's OK – I know you'll have heard about the heart attack by now. You don't have to try and be nice.' He took a deep breath, trying to slow himself. *Stay calm.* 'I've got something to say. It won't take long.'

'Go on,' said Beanie. 'He's listening – we all are.'

Flint drew himself up. 'You and me disagreed, Stretch. About most things probably. I'm not your favourite person. You think I'm stupid, you think I'm full of myself. You think I'm a whole load of stuff – none of it good.' He bit his lip. 'Everyone makes mistakes.'

Stretch's eyes narrowed.

'I've had to do a whole load of thinking,' said Flint. 'You were right about Welbeck. I was dreaming. It was stupid. They didn't want me there. I didn't fit in.'

Stretch allowed himself a wry grin. 'We heard about your little disagreement.'

Flint nodded.

Stretch laughed. 'Wasn't quite how I saw it ending but . . .'

Titters echoed round the room.

'I'm not proud.' Flint held Stretch's gaze. 'I might have been wrong about the club, but not about Janet and Jim. They gave me a new start in life.'

Stretch shrugged, as if to say: So what?

'I might lose that,' said Flint. 'If Jim doesn't get better and stay better, I might have to move back to Bella Gardens.' He shook his head. 'I've had a taste of real life. And I don't want to give it up.'

'*Real* life?' Stretch chuckled.

'Jim put himself out for me,' said Flint. Deep breath. 'Now there's a chance for me to do something for him.' He dropped to his knees. 'I need your help.'

Expressions of astonishment and embarrassment flashed across the faces.

'*All* of you.'

'He's flipped!' Stretch mocked. 'All the stress and worry . . .' He jerked as Beanie dug her elbow sharply into his side. They scowled at each other. 'OK,' growled Stretch, returning his attention to Flint, 'What d'you want?'

'A football team,' said Flint.

Stretch laughed. 'You're winding me up!'

Flint shook his head. 'For Jim to coach. There's a new open challenge tournament. I want us to enter a team. It'll give Jim something to focus on again. The doctor said that might help him recover.'

'But . . .' Stretch's interruption was cut short by another dig in the ribs from Beanie. Again he scowled and she scowled back.

'Why should we?' Nidge's voice.

'What's in it for us?' grunted Stretch.

'You're always bragging about how good you are,' said Flint. 'This is your chance to prove it. If you win, of course, there's the trophy and the prize money. But you'd never pull it off without a coach. Jim is the best.' He got to his feet. 'You've got a few days to think about it. I'll be down the park Sunday morning if you're interested.' At the door he looked back. 'Jim will be there.'

'OK.' Jim clutched the back of the bench. 'Enough.' He eased himself down. 'Half-time . . .' It was a groan. His breath laboured.

'You've done really well,' said Flint.

'Considering.' Jim nodded.

'Come on!' Flint gave an encouraging nudge. 'Two and a half weeks. And already you've doubled your distance.'

Jim nodded. 'And what pace!' He was still breathing in fast little gasps. 'Greased lightning.'

'You mustn't be impatient,' said Flint. 'Dr Richards said it's not going to happen overnight. You have to keep your goals small.'

'Small goals.' Jim half chuckled, half-wheezed. 'Easier to score!'

'That's the idea,' said Flint. 'Speed will come. Until your breathing has recovered, you're bound to be slow. You've got to develop some stamina first. One step at a time.'

'About sums it up!' Jim inhaled slow and deep. 'Mmmm . . .' He breathed out, battling to control the exhalation. 'Tell you what, though . . .' Another breath. '. . . Air never smelt this good.'

Flint smiled, sat back and let his gaze drift. Across the park a dozen or so games of football were being played – some on marked-out pitches with goal posts, others on open ground with cones or litter bins for makeshift goals.

Flint's eyes flitted from one rag-tag game to the next, searching for hints of quality. Boys and men, some in proper kit, others just in jeans and T-shirts, chased the ball in packs, hacking at each other's ankles. Tackles were slow and clumsy, passes came short or too long, shots on goal too high or too hard.

Jim's breathing had calmed. He sighed. 'The beautiful game.'

Flint smiled. 'Spotted a Maradona?' He tried to sound enthusiastic. 'You never know, there might be an undiscovered footballing genius somewhere out there . . .'

'You never know . . .' Jim tutted and shook his head. 'This isn't how things were supposed to turn out. I knew Blanchard would find a way to get rid of me sooner or later.' He tapped his chest. 'Deep down, I think I'd accepted that. But you, you were supposed to be . . .' He shook his head again. 'It's such a waste. Talent needs nurture. It needs challenge.'

'Why not start a new team?' said Flint. 'I could ask around. I might be able to rustle up some players.' His fingers felt for the wood of the bench. He wasn't superstitious, but . . . 'You could train them up, get them into shape, organize them.'

'For what?' Jim's voice was flat. 'Who would we play?'

'Other teams?'

Jim gestured towards the scattered games in front of them. 'From this lot? It's all just casual: groups of mates – neighbours, colleagues, school friends. Any boy with talent will have found himself a club to play with. If you want real competition you'd have to join one of the leagues.'

'The season's nearly over,' said Flint. 'We'd have all summer to sort that out and get prepared.'

Jim sighed. 'You're talking about a proper club with a pitch and kit. That requires money, *serious* money. Something we don't have.' He shook his head. 'We'd be stuck playing casuals in the park.'

Flint frowned. He'd not thought about the practicalities. 'There is another option . . .' He gazed out across the park. *How would Jim take this?* 'We could always go in for the Blanchard Trophy.'

'That's a good one.' Jim chuckled. 'The Blanchard Trophy – I like that! Smart thinking.' He patted Flint's knee. 'Sorry to have to disappoint you old son, but we're too late.'

'Too late?' Flint jerked around. 'We can't be!'

Jim nodded. 'It was on the radio a few days ago. They've stopped taking applications. Got their full quota – most, no doubt, hopeful no-hopers who've scraped the money together. Blanchard will be rubbing his hands with glee.'

Flint stared at the ground. Miserable. *That was it, then?*

'Heave-ho!' With a grunt Jim pushed himself up off the bench. 'Time to head back. Let's not go depressing ourselves. I've enjoyed my little trip today.'

'I could go and see Blanchard,' said Flint. 'Ask him to make an exception. Let us enter.'

'Now you're being foolish.' Jim frowned, then chuckled. Straightening his back, he stretched out his arms. 'Come on. We'll have a little think. We're going further than this tomorrow.'

CHAPTER 20
SUNDAY

Flint was doing his best to ignore the glowering sky. Just his luck. *Today of all days.*

'Just felt a spot of rain.' Jim paused, stuck out his hand and looked up. 'So much for the good old British summer.' He glanced at Flint. 'What d'you reckon?'

'You're doing great this morning,' said Flint, trapping the ball. 'Cracking pace.' He scooped in onto his instep, let it sit dead weight, then flicked it up. Caught it.

A few small scattered groups of boys were kicking footballs, but there was nothing happening near the solitary horse-chestnut that dominated the east side of the park. And no-one underneath it.

Flint rubbed his bare legs. The breeze

had turned sharply colder. 'Let's try and make it to cover.' He nodded towards the giant tree. 'The rain might blow over.'

'My dedicated trainer!' Jim ruffled Flint's hair. 'You're doing an excellent job. Maybe it's the cooler air, but I'm feeling perkier.'

Flint smiled. *Please let them show up.*

Jim pointed back across the park to the bench which, a few days before, had been their resting place before turning back. His finger traced the circumference of the park. 'Must be a good mile from home. And we ain't finished yet.'

As they set off for the tree, rain began to spit, the breeze became gusty.

'Run on ahead,' said Jim. 'No sense us both getting wet.'

'No sense me keeping dry,' said Flint. 'I'm going to be out there in it.' *If anyone turns up.*

'Tough are they, your mates?'

'Yeah,' said Flint. 'You could say that.'

A leaden world: no movement, all colour washed out and drained away by the downpour. Lightning flashed above the rooftops; thunder cracked and rolled across the empty park, rumbling into the distance.

Flint squirmed as a cold trickle splashed down the back of his neck. He checked his watch. Forty minutes solid and still no sign of let-up. The wide tree had kept the rain off till now. But water had worked its way down, saturating the thick foliage. And it was starting to seep through.

'It's slowing!' Jim gestured. 'Looks brighter over there.'

Flint rubbed his arms and hugged himself, trying to shake off his gloom. Was there a difference in the sound? He couldn't hear it. His gaze flitted across the shale sky.

'Hello!' Jim pointed. 'Who's this?'

Flint turned. A small bedraggled group ran splashing through the sodden grass towards them. He counted. *Seven*. The small figure at the front was wearing a red woollen hat. 'Beanie!' He waved.

Thundering in under the branches, Beanie threw herself panting onto the wet ground.

The others laughed as they lumbered behind, collapsed on the grass, or stood clutching themselves, chests heaving.

Seven. Flint peered out into the rain. No sign of any stragglers. Seven was more than he'd expected, less than he had hoped for. Not even enough for five-a-side.

'Jeeeezus, Flint!' Beanie groaned and rolled over onto her back. 'Couldn't you've picked better weather?' She sat up and looked round. 'These are all you get. Some people like a lie-in on Sunday mornings.' Pulling off her hat, she wrung it out and shook the rain from her hair.

Jim chuckled.

Measuring him with her gaze, Beanie smiled and jumped to her feet. 'You must be Jim.' She held out her hand. 'How's it going? Flint's told us about you.'

'It's going very well. Thank you.' Jim shook her hand and nodded to the boys. He grinned. 'Flint assured me a little rain wouldn't deter you.'

'Did he?' Beanie glanced at Flint. 'It's all very well asking everyone to turn up. But guess who's had to go around knocking on people's doors in the pouring rain.' She pulled the hat back on, tugged it down to her ears and tapped herself sharply on the chest. 'That's right! Muggins here. Only three turned up at the house. I went round everyone, but this is all I could drag out.'

'Thanks.' Gutted, Flint forced a smile.

'Listen!' Jim put a hand to his ear.

The rain was slowing.

'Typical!' Beanie scowled. 'I find shelter – the rain stops!'

'And here comes the cavalry!' Grant, a big boy who played in goal, pointed.

Flint turned. Over by the fence more boys were gathered by a gap where railings had been forced aside. Even at a distance he could pick out familiar figures – Stretch was already inside the park and Nidge standing beside him. Flint counted . . . seven, eight, nine . . . another *ten* boys! As the last squeezed through, a crack of clear sky opened above the city. Stretch and his bedraggled band sprinted towards the tree.

'Corner!'

Flint jogged to fetch the ball. The two sides picked by Beanie and Stretch had proved evenly matched. Though nine-a-side with a wet ball on very muddy grass was exhausting, they had kept up a furious pace. He felt utterly knackered, but there was little sign any of the others were flagging. He was impressed. Well impressed. *But would Jim be too? And what would they make of Jim?*

'Come *on*!' squawked Beanie. 'Let's have

all of you into the area, there's only a few minutes left to go.'

Nidge was already there, jostling for space. 'We've been the better side right the way through,' he yelled.

'In your dreams,' chuckled Stretch, attempting to mark him.

Nidge pushed Stretch and moved away. 'Come on!' he yelled to his teammates. 'We can't let Stretch and his bunch of fluky losers beat us.'

'Pride!' roared Stretch in return. 'These no-hopers must not equalize!'

'This corner is our last chance,' yelled Nidge. *'Come on!* We have to make something from it.'

Flint positioned the ball on the ground and paced back surveying the jumble of players. Where to place it? That was the question. For once he didn't care about winning – the other seventeen players had to convince Jim they were good enough to form the basis of a team. Then all he had to do was break it to them about not being able to enter the competition?

As Flint's foot swung up in a satisfying, perfectly executed follow-through, the ball traced an arc just beyond the reach of the jumping players, only dropping as it approached the far post. Waiting patiently out the back, Beanie raced in and dived. A brilliant low header.

'Excellent!' Jumping up from the bench, Jim applauded. 'Fantastic! And a good moment to call it a day, I reckon.' He beckoned. 'Gather over here. Let's have a little chat.'

'Nice one!' Flint patted Beanie on the back.

Beanie grinned. 'Couldn't have done it without you.'

The two mud-splattered teams trudged over to the bench and collapsed on the ground around Jim.

'Where have you lot been hiding?' Jim chuckled. 'I have to confess, when Flint tried to persuade me he knew some players who might be worth watching, I was sceptical.' His eyes sparkled. 'But you were thoroughly entertaining. Look at you, covered from head to foot in mud! Certainly not afraid to get dirty.'

There were titters and mockery as the two teams, now reunited as one group, looked around at one another and took stock.

'I was properly impressed,' said Jim. 'Plenty of talent between you. And nowhere near as raw as I'd expected. Pretty fit too – a bit short of breath maybe, but with training, I'm sure we could create a team to be reckoned with.'

'Does that mean you'd be willing to coach us?' blurted Beanie.

Jim nodded. 'Certainly, I would.'

Flint's heart soared.

'However . . .' Jim frowned. 'I'm afraid you might all be here under a false pretext.'

Puzzled expressions and murmurings rippled round the group.

Jim's eyes fell on Flint.

The Blanchard Trophy. Flint's soaring heart took a nose-dive. With all the excitement and worrying about everything else he had pushed that little problem from his mind. Wearily, he heaved himself up onto his feet. 'When I came to the house the other day I said some stuff about forming a team . . . ?' They were all looking at him. 'About how we might enter the *Sudden Death in July* football challenge?' Heads nodded. 'I didn't realize at the time . . . I'm sorry.' Flint stared at the ground. 'It's not going to be possible.'

More disgruntled murmurings.

'The thing is . . .' Everything had been

going so well. If it hadn't been for the stupid brought-forward closing date . . . There had to be something he could say that would make them stay. 'We could still get a team together.' His voice sounded flat, unconvincing. 'It would be good training. Jim could make big improvements to everyone's game. And . . .' He felt himself floundering. 'And anyway . . .' He knew he was wasting his breath. He knew they wouldn't buy it. What was the point. He had failed. 'I'm sorry you all got out of bed on a rainy Sunday morning for nothing.'

Jim draped an arm across Flint's shoulders. 'He can't be blamed for the mix-up about the competition. The closing date was brought forward. My offer remains – I'd be more than happy to coach you if you want to start training and playing as a team.' His eyes flickered across the muddy players, trying to gauge their mood. 'Who knows – if *Sudden Death in July* is a success, Blanchard might run it again. We could enter it next year.'

Getting to his feet, Stretch stepped forward. 'I don't think any of us is prepared to wait till then.' Muddy nods confirmed. Stretch stared at Flint.

Flint wanted to shout Stretch down, wanted to knock him to the ground and shove mud in his mouth to shut him up. But he knew he couldn't – Stretch was way too strong. And even if he could've, it wouldn't change things.

Beneath the dirt, Stretch's trademark leer was still in place. 'When you came and gave us the big speech about entering the competition, we were inspired, dead impressed weren't we, guys?'

Nods again.

'This might come as a surprise.' Stretch's eyes flickered to Jim. Back to Flint. 'We showed up today because we wanted to get ourselves this brilliant coach you'd been telling us about. You was so fired up – begging for help and unveiling the *masterplan* – you never gave us a chance to tell you.' The leer lengthened into a grin. '*Sudden Death in July* is not a problem . . . we're already registered. We've called ourselves "The Assassins".'

CHAPTER 21
DEAL

Stretch nodded greeting.

Flint sat on the edge of the tatty old sofa next to Beanie. 'Where is everybody?'

'Knackered,' said Stretch. 'Sleeping like babies.'

Flint's gaze flitted around the room. 'Something's different,' he said. 'It struck me before – the place is looking tidier. Smells cleaner too.'

Stretch shrugged.

Beanie chuckled. 'No fag ends. We all packed it in.'

'Everyone?' said Flint.

'We made a pact,' said Stretch. 'No more smokes till the job's over. We're in this thing to win.' Stretching out his long legs, he groaned.

'All of us are a bit stiff,' explained Beanie. 'We've been playing every day since we got the acceptance letter.'

'No wonder you were so impressive on the park.' Flint slumped back into the sofa. Stretch and the gang giving up the fags and starting to train on a daily basis – it was hard to believe. 'I'm lost for words.'

'Money.' Stretch rubbed thumb against fingers. 'We want that prize.'

Flint nodded. 'I should've guessed you weren't doing this on my account.'

'That's where you're wrong.'

'Oh?'

'The big speech was *very* moving,' said Stretch.

Flint scowled at the sarcasm.

'I wanted to interrupt,' said Stretch. 'I was going to tell you we already had the whole thing sorted.'

'Why didn't you?'

'Cos I kept digging him in the ribs,' said Beanie. 'It took a lot of courage for you to come and ask for help like that. I wanted you to have a chance to say what you had to say. It seemed important. You've been through a lot.'

Flint fiddled with a frayed edge. 'So it was just about the money?'

'No.' Stretch frowned. 'Beanie pointed out I . . . *we* still owe you.'

'Owe me?' said Flint.

Stretch nodded.

Flint frowned. 'What for?'

'For not grassing,' said Stretch. 'The shopping trip – remember?'

Flint sat forward. 'You don't *owe* me for that. I was just doing what you or anyone else would do.'

Stretch shrugged. 'You could've lost your chance of being fostered and getting into that stupid football club.'

'It all worked out in the end,' said Flint. 'Well . . .'

'You took the risk,' said Stretch. 'That counts for a lot. So now we're repaying that debt. Besides, like you said, we need Jim's expertise.' He let his gaze drift. 'Your skills might come in handy too.'

'Jim's the man,' said Flint, smiling at Stretch's reluctant compliment. 'But even he can't work miracles.'

Stretch coughed, hacked and leaned

forward. 'Think we don't know that?'

'I'm just saying,' said Flint, 'competition is going to be fierce. We've got the *Sudden Death* to survive before we even get a crack at Welbeck. If we're to have a chance . . .'

'Look, we *want* to win!' Stretch's eyes flashed. 'All right? We're serious about this.' He gave a wry smile. 'We *care*.'

'I want that chance to beat them . . .' Flint thumped the arm of the sofa. '. . . *So* badly! You can't imagine.' He wanted revenge. He wanted to pay Welbeck back for the way they had treated Jim. 'But another thing matters too: if we do this, we have to give it our all. We can't let Jim down.' He held Stretch's gaze. 'It could kill him.'

Stretch shifted uneasily.

'No not turning up for practices,' said Flint. 'No not doing what you're asked . . . no complaining when muscles ache too much, no complaining because you're tired enough to drop, no giving up when it gets too hard and no sabotaging our chances – no thieving, no fighting, no anything else that might blow it.' He licked dry lips. 'Total commitment.'

'Jeeezus!' Stretch frowned. 'All right!'

Flint shook his head. 'Give me your

word.' He held out his hand, palm upwards.

Stretch's eyes narrowed, calculating. He glanced at Beanie. 'OK,' he said, slapping Flint's palm. 'You've got it.'

CHAPTER 22
LAST DAYS

'Maybe I pushed you all a little too hard, yesterday.' Jim sighed wearily. 'Let's give them a few more minutes more before we start.' He leant back against the bench.

Flint turned to where Beanie and the boys stood idly kicking a ball back and forth. They looked tired and dispirited, not exactly enthusiastic to get started. He counted again. *Ten*. Not even enough to field a full team. Things had been going so well all week. But now . . . he was plummeting rapidly towards the pit of despair.

Only three players had dropped out since they started training. They could have coped with that, a squad of fifteen. But now, with only three days to go, this was a devastating blow: *five more missing*.

'Oi-oi!' Beanie pointed. 'Better late than never, I guess.'

Over by the far fence Stretch, Nidge and Grant the goalie were scrambling over the top. Flint scowled. 'I'm going to hurry them up.'

'Hey . . . go easy on them,' warned Jim. 'We don't want any more dropping out. Get them jogging round the park. We'll meet up back under the tree.'

Flint took off across the grass. Clenched fists pumping arms like pistons, legs driving faster and faster till he was sprinting flat out. Furious.

Ambling half-heartedly across the park, Stretch, Nidge and Grant halted and watched his progress. Big Grant grinned.

'What are you smiling for?' Flint staggered to a panting stop. 'You're late!'

Grant glanced at the other two. Stretch and Nidge shrugged. 'Sorry,' said Grant.

'Sorry's a fat lot of use!' snapped Flint. He fought to recover his breath. 'Is that what you'll say when you let the goals in?'

'Leave off him,' said Stretch. 'He's worked as hard as anybody.'

'That's not the point!' Flint glared at

Stretch. 'Everyone's been waiting. You've wasted precious time.'

'We're only half an hour late,' said Stretch. 'You could have started without us.'

Flint stepped up close. 'We had a *deal*.'

Stretch stared back. The muscles in his jaw tightened. 'That's right.' His eyes narrowed. 'Where d'you think we've been? Having a little lie-in?'

'Surprise me.'

Stretch glared.

'Stretch was worried about the numbers,' said Grant.

'We all were,' said Nidge.

'Numbers?' Flint frowned.

'As in dwindling?' Nidge's stare was withering.

'On our way over,' said Grant, 'we called round on the miserable lightweights that've dropped out.' He smacked his fist against his palm. 'We wanted to see if any of them might be persuaded to change their minds, come back and train.'

Flint blushed. He suddenly felt very *stupid*. 'Any luck?'

'Nothing doing.' Stretch kicked at a stick. 'We tried. Sorry.'

Flint glanced at the three boys sheepishly. 'I was out of order.'

'Hey.' Stretch patted him on the back. 'Jim's worked us like dogs the whole week, we're bound to be snappy – we're all knackered.' He almost smiled. 'No hard feelings.'

As the small heavy ball rolled past the cone, Stretch swore loudly.

In his waterproofs and woollen hat, his big clumpy walking boots and thick socks, Flint felt very hot and sweaty, more than a touch irritable and totally ridiculous. He took small comfort from knowing he wasn't the only one.

'OK,' Jim yelled from the bench. 'Let's take a breather. Have a good long drink from your water bottles. Don't want you all burning up. You can take off your hats.'

'Wimps!' Beanie grinned and made a rude gesture as the boys flung their head gear on the ground. For once in her life, she hadn't looked out of place.

'I know you're exhausted,' said Jim, 'but this is the toughest it gets. It's just going to be gentle stuff between now and Saturday. After what I've put you through today, the tournament will feel like a holiday.'

Stretch groaned. 'If any of us survive.'

Jim chuckled and clapped his hands. 'Right, Grant and the back four – let's have Flint and Nidge playing attack for you. I'm not expecting you to score goals. But, more importantly, I don't want to see any being let in. The rest of you, attackers and midfielders, your job is to try and put one or more past them. Got it?'

The players dispersed into their separate teams and took up positions. Jim blew his whistle.

Nidge's pass curved just beyond Flint's reach. He accelerated. Fellow midfielder, Rankin, now the enemy, trapped the ball and tapped it across to Stretch.

'Go on, Flint!' Beanie's voice, somewhere off to the left, cut through the other shouts and yells. 'Take it off him!'

Flint shook the sweat from his eyes. In front of him, Stretch jiggled the ball between his feet, inviting a challenge, weighing up the options. The leer was back. Flint ignored it and watched for telltale signs: a furtive glance or dropping shoulder – which way would Stretch go?

'A couple more minutes!' yelled Jim. 'Come on defenders, you're doing an excellent job. Keep that ball *out*!'

Stretch twisted left. With a grunt, Flint lunged, stabbing the ball with his toe. Their shoulders crashed, bodies ground one against the other, as they fought to push ahead. Edging in front, Flint felt Stretch's grasp and a sharp tug on his sleeve. He jerked, wrenched himself free and poked again with the toe of his clumsy boot.

The ball flew to cocky toughnut Clifton, a harrier on the right as fierce as Beanie on the left. Carlton's twin, Clifton had been there that day in the shopping mall, dodging and weaving through the crowds with the best of them. Now, showing the same skill and agility, he ran past one player and barged another. Skipping tackle after tackle, he created panic. But finally, hemmed in, he slammed on the brakes and backheeled.

'You gave it away!' yelled Jim. 'Right – come on, attackers! One minute. You've got the ball. Let's have that goal!'

Rankin was back in possession, legs churning, pushing past Nidge.

Flint raced back to join the defenders. It was too much! Every muscle screamed for rest.

The ball was in the air. 'Come *on*!' Grant

edged out from the goal, big gloved hands at the ready. *'Get rid of it!'*

Stretch charged. Beanie scuttled out to meet him, low and dangerous. Tackling with lightning speed, she put the ball into the air.

'Mine!' Flint's lungs seared as he yelled. Chesting the ball, he brought it under control with his foot. But, out of nowhere, Rankin jumped in front of him and popped it up again. Stretch leapt for it. Grant did the same. Colliding in mid-air, they fell.

Jim's whistle blew. Full time.

The ball rolled to a stop on the goal line.

'Excellent!' yelled Jim. 'Excellent – all of you. Couldn't have been better. You did yourselves proud.'

Rubbing their bruises, Grant and Stretch crawled to their feet.

Flint staggered. Dizzily he tugged at his layers of shirts, struggling to drag them up over his head. His legs shook like jelly; his whole body felt numbed. Other players fought with their clothing, desperate to get cool air to cooked bodies.

'Hey!' Laughter rang clear across the park. 'The circus came early this year!'

Flint span. The voice – distinctive, sneering, familiar – he knew that voice.

More laughter. 'Look! A troop of clowns!'

Over by the main road, near the side gate on the far side of the fence, a small group had gathered. With the sun behind them, it was impossible to make out faces, but Flint didn't need to see. The voice was unmistakable. *Aldo Blanchard.*

'Hey! And the funny old man too!'

'Do some tricks for us, clowns!'

'Come on, funny old man. Let's see you perform!'

'Careful you don't keel over!'

With a final furious tug, Stretch wrenched his sweat-soaked shirts over his head and flung them at the ground. 'Clowns, is it? Who are these jokers?'

Jim waved a dismissive hand. 'Ignore them.'

But Stretch was already striding towards the fence. 'Clowns – yeah?'

Struggling to remove layers of shirts and jackets, Nidge, Clifton and Beanie set off behind them. The rest of the squad followed.

'Lads!' Jim waved his arms in vain.

'Hey!' Flint tried to run, but leaden legs would not oblige.

'Oi, you!' Stretch advanced towards the fence, stabbing the air with his index finger. 'Yes, you with the big mouth and the stupid voice!' He shook his fist. 'Looking to make something of it?'

Aldo laughed. Behind him some of his friends were edging back towards the fence. 'I thought clowns were supposed to have a sense of humour!'

Stretch broke into a trot. 'I'll give you something to laugh about!'

'Oh dear!' Aldo mocked. 'Coco's getting annoyed.'

Stretch charged. Nidge, Clifton and Beanie broke into a run.

'Stretch!' Flint forced his legs to move faster.

Aldo glanced back to where his friends were retreating through the gate.

Stretch tore towards him, snarling.

'I don't think he likes me!' yelped Aldo.

Stretch was ten metres and closing.

'Ooops!' Aldo turned and fled. In a flash he was through the entrance.

As the gate clanged shut, Stretch crashed, yelling, into its steel bars. 'You little...'

On the other side, one of Aldo's mates slammed the bolt home, another rammed a stick through the slot, jamming it shut. Grinning at Stretch, Aldo wagged a finger.

'Temper, temper!' Behind him his mates jeered and mocked.

Stretch kicked at the stick, but it was shielded by the bars. He grabbed the bars and shook the gate. 'You snot-faced little cowards!'

Nidge, Clifton and Beanie shook their fists and hurled insults.

'Stretch!' Staggering, panting to a halt, Flint lunged for his arm. But Stretch shrugged him off and began clambering up the gate. Flint grabbed again. 'Stretch! Leave it!'

'Well, I never! Our ruffian ex-teammate!' Aldo smirked. 'Should have known you'd be hanging round with the old invalid and his band of street urchins.'

Flint glared.

Aldo gestured towards Stretch, jerking and twisting as he tried to break free of Flint's grip. The smirk widened. 'Looks like you finally found your level.'

'Go on, Stretch!' yelled Clifton.

'Do him!' yelled Carlton.

'Just like the zoo!' chuckled Aldo, pointing. 'This lot aren't clowns . . .' He made a rhythmical grunting sound. 'They're *apes*!'

Flint yanked hard, tugging Stretch away from the gate.

179

'Get your hands off me!' snarled Stretch, grabbing Flint's collar. 'What's wrong with you?' He thrust his face up close. 'Where's your self-respect?'

Flint glared back. 'They're Welbeck.'

'What!?' Stretch's face darkened. 'All the more reason to give them a good kicking!'

'No!'

'You're just going to let them rubbish Jim and slag off the rest of us?'

'Yes!' hissed Flint. 'And so are you.' His eyes blazed. 'No sabotaging our chances. *You gave me your word.*'

Clifton, Nidge, Beanie and the rest fell silent, watching.

Stretch's face twitched.

Flint pointed back across the park, towards Jim. 'Come on, walk away from this. *Now.*'

Scowling furiously, Stretch released his grip on Flint's collar. Without a glance at Aldo and his braying mob, he spat towards the fence, twisted away and headed off across the park. Shoulders hunched, the others followed; a defeated army.

'You don't have a hope!' yelled Aldo. 'You and your dumb roughneck friends. Come off it! Save yourselves a humiliation at the weekend.'

'Careful, Aldo.' Flint stepped up to the fence, his voice steady and low. 'Your fear's showing.'

Aldo snorted. 'You'll be knocked out in the first round.'

'You'd better hope so,' said Flint, 'because if we meet you, we're gonna beat you. You and your daddy are going to get the thrashing you deserve.'

'Dream on.'

Flint turned to follow his teammates. 'See you on the park.'

CHAPTER 23
SUDDEN DEATHS

Under a bright, summer morning sun, the air shimmered with anticipation. It was the day. And it was quite something. Flint couldn't think of another occasion when he'd experienced such an atmosphere. So many football teams in one place! So many different strips, such an array of different colours and designs – thirty-three squads including Welbeck, who had turned up already to watch the early rounds. Hundreds of players. With parents, coaches, hangers on and supporters, there had to be several thousand people.

The carnival throng buzzed with nervousness, cameraderie and bravado. Anxious eyes darted, assessing potential opposition. Players laughed away their tension, joked to buoy confidence. Necks craning, hands cupped to ears, the expectant teams and their coaches crowded round the organizers, awaiting instructions, eager to get started.

The ball came soaring. Flint glanced around checking positions, maneouvred himself into its flight-path, then leapt to meet it. His neat powerful header flew out towards the touchline.

'Nice!' With the ball at his feet Nidge took off running, up the wing.

'Good work in the midfield!' yelled Jim from the touchline. 'Push up – keep the pressure on!'

Flint raced into the opposition half. Ahead of him, Stretch lengthened his stride. His two previous shots had required lightning fast reactions from the goalie; this time the blue-shirted Middleton defenders moved straight in to neutralize the danger.

Nidge accelerated.

'Go on!' yelled Jim. 'Give 'em a run for their money!'

Flint had found himself a good space. He whistled and waved. 'Nidge!'

The right-back lunged. Nidge side-stepped and flicked the ball.

With a run and a jump, Flint volleyed it deep into the penalty area.

Players crowded in. Stretch's head rose above the others, jerking with the impact.

Victory could be as simple as that.

Tackling a Queenstown striker on the edge of the box, Beanie broke free with the ball and whacked it with all her strength. It travelled more than half the pitch and landed within a metre of Flint. Three yellow-shirted defenders stood between him and their goalie.

'Flint!'

'Flint!'

Shooting past him, Rankin on the inside, Carlton on the outside, surged towards the goal. Flint chipped to Carlton.

Head bobbing, Carlton powered as far as he could take it then slipped the ball across to Rankin.

Flint accelerated through the scattered defenders. Rankin flicked it up. Leaping through the keeper's arms, Flint brought the ball down like a bullet.

'GOOOOAL!'

* * *

Flint and Stretch raced each other towards the goal, outstripping a retreating midfield, penetrating the defence.

On the wing, Nidge kept pace, glancing across for the perfect moment. Without pausing he passed. The ball floated in over the heads of frantic defenders.

Though the goalie rushed out, Stretch's head nudged the ball beyond his reach. Flint's half-volley shook the crossbar. And Rankin thundered in to tap the rebound home.

Beanie crossed to Clifton.

Spotting a gap, Clifton took off up the touchline, right-back turned winger. Carlton signalled. Clifton dummied to him but fed the ball to Nidge.

Bringing it forward, Nidge delivered to Carlton. Stretch and Flint dodged their markers and found space as Carlton zigzagged, drawing defenders away from the centre. Finally, hemmed in, he backheeled. Ready and waiting, Rankin lobbed. Defenders span too late. With another perfect header, Stretch had put them out of the competition.

* * *

Everything hung on the smallest of turns.

Confident from their string of victories, Banberry pushed hard. But, with a sliding tackle, Beanie stole the ball from their captain. She twisted to keep it. Twisted again to slip it out to Flint.

And suddenly they were charging three abreast towards enemy territory. Flint, Stretch and Rankin crossed at a sprint into Banberry's half, passing the ball deftly between them. One more win and they'd be the Sudden Death winners, through to the final – and the longed-for face-off against Aldo and the boys.

'Get back!' Banberry's coach ordered his midfield to meet the danger.

'Tackle!' yelled their captain.

But Flint, Stretch and Rankin ploughed on, evading tackles and eating up the turf.

With his path blocked, Flint tapped the ball to Rankin. *'Go on!* Take a shot.'

Cries of *'Shoot!'* went up from the touch-line.

Switching directions, Rankin cut across the front of the goal, swerved last minute and blasted.

The deflection caught a defender's arm. The ball dropped. Flint stepped in and buried it.

* * *

Exhilaration... pride... relief... resolve... apprehension... *exhaustion*... snapped through a camera's lens, these expressions and more were captured on the faces of The Assassins as they left the field at the end of their fifth encounter. The photographer from the local paper, satisfied perhaps that he had images worthy of the back page, glanced at his watch and headed off towards the refreshment kiosk.

Rubbing aching muscles, Flint watched the man with envy. An hour to kill before the big final, time to grab a Coke and bag of chips and maybe take a stroll... if only! He and his teammates had an hour to *recover*. After five hard-fought contests, just one hour to find the strength for the biggest fight of their lives – a sixty-minute match against fresh and rested Welbeck.

CHAPTER 24
JOY AND PAIN

Welbeck and their supporters roared with delight.

Aldo, pursued by his jubilant teammates, ran back towards his own half, punching the air in celebration of his second goal. 'This is too easy!' he yelled. 'Come on, clowns!' He jabbed a mocking finger towards Flint and his weary dejected teammates. 'Forgotten how to play? Lost your bottle?'

Surrounded by cheering Welbeck supporters, Blanchard and Llewellyn exchanged congratulatory nods.

'Come on, Welbeck! Finish them off before half-time!'

'Assassins! Pull one back!'

Cheers and shouts filled the air from both sides. Flint glanced down at the crowded touchline. The Assassins had brought few supporters of their own. But many of those who had come along to cheer their own teams through the knockout rounds had stayed to watch the final, intrigued to see how Jim's scruffy-looking outfit would perform. Judging by the shouts of encouragement, much of that crowd were getting behind them. The underdogs.

'Keep your nerve!' yelled Jim.

Flint watched his exhausted teammates shuffling back towards the centre. Was Jim's plan working? Welbeck had been forced to work really hard – but they'd still managed to score. They had been tiring, making mistakes and committing fouls – their frustration had been heading towards breaking point. But now they'd scored a second goal, their spirits had been suddenly lifted. The Assassins looked defeated.

'Come on. Keep soaking it up!' yelled Jim. 'Just a few minutes more.'

'That's right, you saps!' Aldo's mocking laughter rang out across the pitch. 'Keep soaking it up like the punchbags you are.'

'I've had enough.' Stretch scowled. 'Soaking it up!' He spat. 'Look at them! Welbeck and their supporters are laughing at us. It's time we showed them.'

'Yeah!' growled Nidge.

'A goal would be nice,' said Rankin. 'It'd give us a lift.'

Beanie nodded. 'How about it, you guys?'

There were nods and grunts of agreement from the other nearby players.

'It's too early,' said Flint. 'You heard what Jim said – if we go on the offensive now we'll burn ourselves out before the break. Then Welbeck will walk all over us.'

Stretch sneered. 'Which they aren't doing already?'

'We've worked our guts out all day,' said Flint. 'They've just been standing around watching. We have to keep wearing them down. There's no other way we're going to win that trophy. Don't let them get to you. That's just what they want.'

'Assassins?' mocked Aldo. 'Deadbeats more like!'

'It's not about prizes or glory any more,' snarled Stretch. 'It's about pride. This is personal. I'm not taking this taunting any longer. There's only one way to silence these dirtbags . . .'

Nidge shook a fist. 'By going on the attack!'

Stretch nodded. 'There isn't long to half-time. I say we hit back hard – now! They think we're already whipped. Let's knock the stuffing out of them!'

Placing the ball on the centre spot, Stretch waited for his team to take up their positions.

The whistle blew. Stretch charged. Passing rapidly and pushing forward, The Assassins advanced at a furious pace.

Welbeck were caught off guard with midfield players too far forward and defenders wrong-footed. 'Get back,' yelled Aldo, retreating at a sprint. 'Mark your man. Tackle!'

On the wing, Nidge had already slipped behind the back four.

With the forwards and the rest of the midfield deep into enemy territory, Flint had little choice but to follow. Stretch was on the edge of the box; four more Assassins had arrived in the penalty area when Nidge found the space to get in a cross.

It came floating low. Carlton dived. The keeper parried the ball skyward with both fists. Players leapt, but it sailed above their heads. From the edge of the box, Carlton volleyed wildly.

The ball ricocheted, a defender fell, another tried to clear the rebound, but Stretch beat him to it and, in a flash, was darting towards the goal. Another shot. Orange shirts threw themselves and the goalie dived. The ball rolled outside the post. Blowing his whistle, the referee pointed for a corner.

'Goal!' 'Corner!' 'Foul!' 'Hand-ball!' Players waved protesting hands. The crowd bayed its opinions.

'Hand-ball!' yelled Stretch.

'Don't be ridiculous!' Aldo laughed.

'You fisted it off the line!' Red-faced with fury, Stretch strode towards him.

'Desperado!' taunted Aldo, rubbing his eyes as if crying. 'Sad clown!'

Flint ran. Stretch shoved Aldo. Grinning, Aldo taunted. Stretch's fist swung. Aldo ducked. The referee stepped in.

'Stretch!' Flint grabbed his arms.

'Get your hands off me!' Stretch jerked and tugged to break free. Other players charged in to intervene.

The referee blew his whistle. A linesman came running. The two men conferred. Stony-faced, the referee produced a red card for Stretch. 'Your game is over, son.' He pointed. 'Off!'

Flint felt Stretch shake with rage.

Glancing at his watch, the referee blew his whistle again. 'Half-time!' he barked. 'Back to the changing rooms all of you. And let's, everybody, try to *cool off and calm down!*'

'I'm sorry.' Stretch looked at the floor.

Flint glanced around the changing room – heads hung in postures of dejection.

'Don't be too hard on yourselves,' said Jim. 'This is a tough one.'

'I can't believe I did that.' Stretch shook his head. 'I can't believe I let him get to me . . .'

'He does that,' said Flint.

'From where I was standing it was clearly a hand-ball,' said Jim. 'But we have to put all that behind us. There's still everything to play for – a game to be won.'

Heads lifted wearily.

'You've played brilliantly,' said Jim. 'And apart from the last few minutes when things got a touch frantic, you kept your heads. You did what I'd asked. Well done! Now we have to talk about how we're going to win this thing.'

'Now we go on the attack!'

'We'll still need to pace ourselves,' said Jim. 'We need to conserve energy when we can. Having said that, Welbeck were really forced to use themselves up in that first half. We can look forward to a much fairer fight.'

'If it wasn't for the fact that we've only got ten men,' said Nidge.

Jim shook his head. 'We're the underdogs. We can make that into a big psychological advantage. Welbeck have everything to lose. We've got everything to win. The crowd are getting behind us and after that disallowed handball and Aldo's show of petulance, they're even more on our side.'

'Hey, Flint!'

Heading back to the pitch, Flint jerked round.

'Congratulations!'

'*Congratulations?*' Flint smiled, recognizing Dr Richards. 'You're joking aren't you? We're two–nil down.'

Richards chuckled. 'Ah, yes! But it's a game of two halves remember. Actually, I was referring to your having got a team together. You've done it so quickly. Jim looks fantastic. I've just had the results of his tests and they're excellent.' He held out his hand. 'You should take some credit.'

'Heh!' Flint shook Richards's hand. 'Then so should you!'

Richards smiled. 'Quite a team.'

Flint nodded. 'So are this lot.' He gestured towards his teammates, filing out onto the pitch. 'They've worked like dogs.'

'You've got the coach,' said Richards. 'And the tactics. You're certainly not lacking motivation.'

'But now we're down to ten men,' said Flint. 'It's going to be tough . . . really tough.'

'My money's on The Assassins.' Richards bared his teeth and made a fist. 'Fighting back! The crowd are with you now. They're going to be urging you on to victory.'

'We'll need it,' said Flint.

'You mark my words,' said Richards. 'Everyone loves a team coming from behind.'

Flint spotted a flash of orange as the first of Welbeck started to make their way back onto the pitch. He felt himself tensing. 'We've got something to prove,' he muttered. 'We *have* to win.'

Richards nodded. 'Winning is what it's

all about, of course. But, whatever the outcome, you should be proud: you've already won an important victory — Jim has a team to coach and a future to look forward to, I've no doubt that's been the key to his recovery.'

'Thanks.' Flint smiled and nodded towards the pitch. 'I have to go.'

'Give it your best shot.'

It hadn't been all their own way, not by any means. Welbeck had come out from half-time, attacking with ferocity. They wanted to bury The Assassins and have done with it — to prove the point, they had even managed a third goal. But Jim's stamina-training and tactics had paid off. The heat had done the rest. Just ten minutes into the second half, Flint had pulled one back with a twenty-yard shot. Now Welbeck were starting to wilt.

'ASS-ASS-INS! ASS-ASS-INS!'

'Come on The Assassins!'

The cheering and chanting were electrifying. There was no doubting who the crowd wanted to win. Welbeck's home following were all but drowned out by Assassins' supporters.

With a shrill whistle, Clifton passed

forward to his brother. Slamming on the brakes, Carlton made a swift change of direction, deftly wrong-footing his marker.

Flint sprinted into open space, signalling for the ball. It was an incredible feeling: out of nowhere, the phoenix of confidence rising from the ashes. Slowly but surely, The Assassins had clawed their way into the light. *'Man on!'*

Carlton's perfect pass arrived. Flint glanced around, checking the positions of his teammates. Consistently The Assassins were out-running their markers and beating tackles. They passed with easy accuracy, read each other's minds, anticipated and thwarted the opposition's moves. They were playing like champions.

Flint waited as Aldo and Moses closed to tackle; he flicked the ball wide to Rankin and pushed forward. Skipping Aldo's clumsy attempt to chop him, he sped towards the Welbeck goal. A short distance ahead, Rankin had already delivered to Nidge.

Powering up the wing, Nidge slowed towards the corner and hesitated. One defender was on his case, a second on his way, others glanced nervously as Flint,

Rankin and Carlton, avenging angels, thundered in.

Effortlessly evading the first tackle, Nidge twisted and passed back before the second defender could reach him. Right where she was needed, Beanie met the ball with a perfect volley. Rankin headed, Carlton chested and chipped, Flint swerved and blasted at the top corner.

'Goooal!'

'Beauty!'

The crowd erupted.

It was in the net. Scowling, the keeper turned to collect the ball.

'Ass-ass-ins! Ass-ass-ins!'

In Stretch's absence, Flint, leading from the front, had run, tackled, passed, encouraged, shot, headed, harried, crossed, chased, run, shot, passed, run . . . faster, better, stronger than ever before. With two shiny goals under his belt, he could taste victory and vindication on the hot summer air. Punching the air triumphantly, he raced back to his own half, pursued by cheering, jubilant teammates.

On the touchline, Llewellyn's voice had fallen silent. Now Blanchard barked the orders. Welbeck were resorting to a rearguard action – every player pulled back to defend the remaining minutes. It was a desperate attempt to hang on to their one-goal lead. For flagging Welbeck, extra time promised certain doom.

'Come on! The game's not over yet!' Echoing his father's commands, Aldo strove to put backbone into his faltering soldiers. 'Keep possession at all costs! We're *not* letting these clowns steal our glory.'

Welbeck's kick. Passing back from the centre, they moved the ball around frenetically. But they were too eager to get rid of the ball. Their confidence, like their energy, was sapped – no-one wanted to be responsible for losing possession. Assassins charged forward: marauders.

From out of nowhere hurtled Beanie. She flung herself to intercept a lazy pass: slid along the turf and chopped the ball.

'Nice one!' Flint dashed to collect. 'OK. Let's do it!'

Rankin, Carlton and Nidge set off at a run. Back on her feet, Beanie followed behind.

Flint dodged and swerved, advancing the ball through Welbeck's lines. Accelerating. *'Ass-ass-ins!'* roared the crowd. *'One more goal!'* He felt exhilarated, thirsty for a third goal, the magic hat trick. His kick was perfectly timed, the arc of the long pass low and beautiful. This must be what athletes meant when they talked of being *in the zone*. '*One more goal!*' repeated the crowd. One more goal meant extra time and victory almost guaranteed – Welbeck were a beaten team.

With two Welbeck players closing in, Carlton played safe and punted the ball back to his brother. Fired up by the chanting, Clifton sprinted down the touch-line.

Jim, Janet and Sandra cheered with the rest of the supporters. Stretch was there too, leaping up and down and yelling like a maniac beside him. Beside him, Dr Richards appeared a touch more restrained.

'Get forward!' Flint turned and beckoned to his defenders. 'It's all or nothing time!' As he ran, Dr Richards's words came back to him: the team was vital to Jim's recovery. *But victory meant the end.* Stretch and the gang would split their prize-money and disappear. Victory meant no more team. All over. Dr Richards had said a future to look forward to was the vital thing. Flint staggered to a halt. If they defeated Welbeck, it was Jim who would be the loser.

Hemmed in, Clifton slipped the ball to Beanie.

Beanie charged.

'Get stuck in!' Aldo's shrill yell cut through the crowd's roar. 'Come *on*, you pussies! *Stop her!*'

Flint shook himself and sprinted. His head was churning, calculating as he ran. He so badly wanted to defeat Welbeck, so badly wanted to do something that would hurt Aldo and Blanchard. But Stretch was hell-bent on beating Aldo too and if The Assassins lost today there was only one way he could do that – *keep the team together for a rematch* . . .

'Flint!' The pass from Beanie came straight to his feet.

'Come on, Assassins!' roared the supporters. *'One more goal!'*

Flint backheeled to Rankin and cut sideways into a gap.

Charging forward, Rankin chipped it back.

As Flint crossed the line into the crowded penalty area, it seemed like every Welbeck player was there to block his course.

'Get the BALL!' Red-faced Aldo yelled and pointed. 'STOP him!'

Flint passed wide to Nidge and looked for space. Nidge sped forward, twisted and returned to sender. Now Flint was in the thick, dodging and swerving. Aldo did his best to block, but Flint dummied, grinned and slipped the ball through his legs to Carlton.

Unable to find a way past the defenders, Carlton chipped it back. 'Yours!'

Flint pushed forward. The ball kept returning to him, as if the outcome of this final struggle insisted on being his choice, his responsibility . . . his *destiny*. He barged a path through ex-teammates, looking for the goal. He twisted, lurched, skipped a scything tackle and turned. Suddenly he was there, in the clear, with only the keeper between him and the net. It was his call. And he knew what he had to do.

Glancing up at the blue sky above the crossbar, he blasted . . .

It was largely Welbeck supporters who had stayed to watch Blanchard hand the trophy to his son. Much of the crowd had drifted away before the prize ceremony began. The wrong side had won. Janet, Sandra, Dr Richards, Jim, Flint and the rest of the squad stood with the remains of their supporters, trying to ignore Welbeck's triumphalist chants and derisory taunting.

Turning away, Jim glanced towards Flint. 'If I had a pound for every time I've warned a player to keep their heads down when they're shooting . . .' he sighed, 'I'd probably be a millionaire by now.'

'Yeah.' Stretch scowled. 'Shame someone didn't listen to that advice, we might all have been a little richer.'

Flint bowed his head. Guilt not shame.

'I hardly think the boy who gets sent off in the first half is in any position to blame teammates for defeat,' said Jim. 'Call me biased, but Flint gets my vote for man of the match.'

'Mine too!' Carlton patted Flint on the back. 'You played like a dream, mate.' Cheers of agreement echoed Carlton's sentiment.

Jim turned to Stretch. 'Everyone's allowed the occasional mistake, eh? Sorry to disappoint you, but as far as having been richer goes, the rules of the competition stated quite clearly: prize money gets paid into the winning team's bank account. There were strict conditions about what it gets spent on.' He chuckled. 'I don't recall seeing anything about presents or pocket money for players.'

Beanie gave Stretch a shove. 'Told you you should have read that stuff!'

Stretch glared. 'It wasn't about the money.' He pointed to the celebrating Welbeck players. 'We came here to show those jokers who was boss.' His face dropped. 'And we *failed*. But that won't happen next time.'

'Next time?' said Flint.

'We're going to train harder than ever,' said Stretch. 'We're going to train with Jim every single day. We're going to apply to join the league.'

Flint felt his heart float.

'Whether it's two months down the line, or a year from now . . .' Stretch clenched his fist. '. . . Next time we meet Welbeck we're taking them to the cleaners!'

Beanie cupped hands to mouth. 'Next time we'll take you to the cleaners!' She chanted to the tune of a football song. 'Next time we'll show you how it's done!' Others joined in. Welbeck and their supporters looked awkward and uncomfortable. The chorus grew louder and louder.

'You won't have a chance!' yelled Stretch. 'Even when you had every advantage, we nearly destroyed you. You won't be so lucky next time.'

'Great team spirit, your bunch of ruffians!' Flint turned. Dr Richards emerged from the crowd. 'You in particular – fantastic game, unbelievable in the second half.' The doctor had to shout to make himself heard above the chanting. 'Jim's a lucky man.'

'We lost,' said Flint.

'Indeed,' said Richards. 'That final shot.' He leant close. 'Good call!'

'What!?' Flint blushed. But the look in Richards's eye left no doubt: he had sussed – he knew it had been no mistake. He *knew*.

'Hey!' Sandra emerged from the jumping, chanting mêlée. Janet and Jim followed behind. 'Never mind,' said Sandra ruffling Flint's hair. 'You played your best. That's what counts.'

Jim nodded. 'Terrific.'

'You mustn't feel bad about one little error,' said Janet.

'That's what I've just been telling him.' Dr Richards winked.

Flint sighed. 'I guess even great players have days when they miss.'

THE END

FLINT
Neil Arksey

*Imagine being a talented footballer –
yet never being allowed to play . . .*

No football – ever. That's the deal Flint
has with his dad, a bad-tempered
bully with a dodgy back and an
even dodgier means of earning a
living – as a petty thief.

But nothing can keep Flint from playing
football for long. And when he is offered a
place in a local team, suddenly Dad no
longer seems to mind! Flint's over the
moon – until he realizes what Dad's
real motives are . . .

A tough, hard-hitting and action-packed
football tale.

From the author of *Brooksie*.

ISBN 0 440 864208

CORGI YEARLING BOOKS

BROOKSIE
Neil Arksey

Imagine being the son of one of England's top strikers ... Great, yes?

No! Not if, like Lee Brooks, your dad – 'Brooksie' – has suddenly lost form and become the laughing-stock of the whole country.

Lee hates Brooksie for letting him down. And Lee hates having to move to a grotty new home without his dad. With his own on-pitch confidence at an all-time low, he even begins to hate *football*. But then he meets Dent and his mates and the chance is there for him to play again – with a team of seriously talented players. They've just one problem – no pitch!

A cracking football tale, filled with goal-scoring action and dramatic matchplay moments.

ISBN 0 440 863813

CORGI YEARLING BOOKS

All Transworld titles are available by post from:

Bookpost
PO Box 29
Douglas
Isle of Man IM99 1BQ

Tel: +44(0)1624 836000
Fax: +44(0)1624 837033
Internet http://www.bookpost.co.uk
or e-mail: bookshop@enterprise.net

Free postage and packing in the UK.
Overseas customers: allow £1 per book (paperbacks) and £3 per book (hardbacks).